The Beginners

ALSO BY ANNE SERRE

The Fool and Other Moral Tales
The Governesses

The Beginners

Anne Serre

translated from the French
by Mark Hutchinson

A NEW DIRECTIONS PAPERBOOK ORIGINAL

Originally published in French as *Les Débutants*

First published as New Directions Paperbook 1507 in 2021
Manufactured in the United States of America
Design by Erik Rieselbach

Library of Congress Cataloging-in-Publication Data
Names: Serre, Anne, 1960– author. |
Hutchinson, Mark (Translator), translator.
Title: The beginners / Anne Serre ; translated from the French
by Mark Hutchinson.
Other titles: Débutants. English
Description: New York : New Directions Publishing Corporation, 2021.
Identifiers: LCCN 2021001805 | ISBN 9780811230315 (paperback ;
acid-free paper) | ISBN 9780811230322 (ebook)
Classification: LCC PQ2679.E67335 D4313 2021 | DDC 843/.914—dc23
LC record available at https://lccn.loc.gov/2021001805

10 9 8 7 6 5 4 3 2 1

New Directions Books are published for James Laughlin
by New Directions Publishing Corporation
80 Eighth Avenue, New York 10011

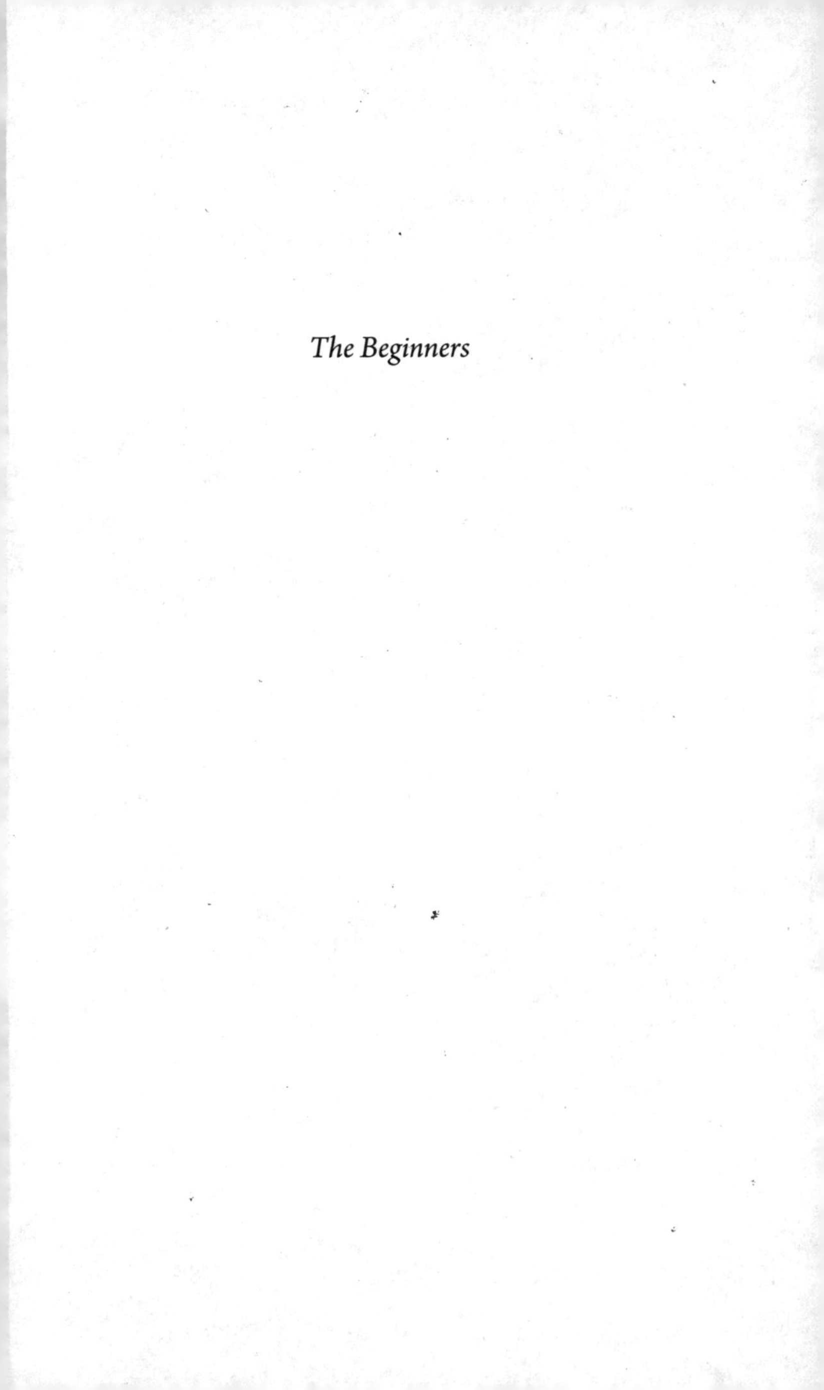

The Beginners

IN AUGUST 2002, ANNA LORE, age forty-three, fell madly in love with Thomas, age fifty-six. For twenty years, Anna had been living with Guillaume Ruys, she loved him and he loved her, they didn't have children but Anna didn't want any, and Guillaume already had two from a previous relationship. Their life was happy and had never come up against the deadweight of boredom or routine, they still made passionate love, traveled from time to time, seldom quarreled, he was an architect, she wrote for art magazines, she had a childlike trust in him, he looked on her as a marvel.

On August 6, 2002, in a street in Sorge, the small town of some ten thousand inhabitants in which they lived, Anna saw a man coming toward her whom she recognized vaguely and whose name she almost knew. Tall and slim, Thomas Lenz had stooped forward slightly to greet her, for there was something he wished to say to her. The space around Anna had changed. He wanted to congratulate her on an article of hers he had read and was taking the liberty of doing so, he said, because the article was on display in the window of the local bookstore. He had no intention of striking up a conversation with her, he would later explain, he was just being polite and friendly to a woman he knew by name and had already seen passing by in the street. Other than that she wrote for an art magazine which he bought from time to time, he knew nothing about her or her life.

They stood talking for a while, as you do when you meet someone in the street in summer, and it's sunny out and you're in no great hurry, and Thomas moreover was on vacation. They talked about art, and since they were standing outside a café, they went and sat down on the terrace to pursue their conversation. But the damage was already done, for both of them. Anna knew this at once; Thomas was dimly aware of a peculiar feeling, but as he wasn't much given to introspection, thought nothing more of it. He would later explain that he hadn't even found her especially pretty. He had found her charming and, above all, interesting. He had enjoyed chatting with her.

He wasn't conscious of anything yet, but the following day at the same time he was back at the same spot, as was Anna. Again they had coffee and talked about art. Anna felt very comfortable in his presence. After all, she said to herself, it's a pleasant conversation, of no great importance; and besides, it's nice to have someone new to talk to. In reality, she was already strongly attracted to him and had been from the moment she'd set eyes on him, but she brushed that away into a corner at the back of her mind. She didn't tell Guillaume about the meeting, and then she did tell him: "I had a coffee with Thomas Lenz—you know, the research scientist, he's very nice." In Guillaume's heart, since he knew Anna by heart, there was a small explosion. He ignored it, resumed what he'd been doing, and, from that day forth, began making love to her much more frequently and rather more ardently than in previous months, and things carried on like this, as we shall see, for a whole year.

A few days later, though it was raining and the temperature had fallen sharply, Anna and Thomas again ran into each other at the same time and the same place. I'll say no, she said to herself. He came over and asked her if she'd like a coffee. She said no. He would later claim to have found her distinctly frosty and to have been a bit annoyed by this. Once again, when the sun had come back out, they found themselves at the same spot; she invented a reason for not staying longer. Then one day, while she was walking in the countryside with her sister a few miles from Sorge, Thomas suddenly appeared on the path, accompanied by a child, and once again coming straight toward her. He would later explain that, during their second conversation at the café, she had mentioned that she liked to go walking over by that village from time to time; and he didn't know why, but on that particular day he'd felt like going for a walk there, too, and a nephew of his had tagged along.

Again he found her icy. In reality, the coincidence astounded her. She was also embarrassed, because she had been arguing with her sister when he turned up and was afraid he might have seen her face looking strained and unpleasant and heard her speaking bluntly. When the moment came to shake hands and say goodbye, there was such a confusion of outstretched hands—her sister's, his nephew's, Thomas's, her own—that they ended up shaking hands in a most peculiar fashion, a bit like the way you make a seat for someone by locking your arms together: fumbling about, but quite obviously searching for each other.

He reminded her of someone, but she didn't know

who. And that impossible memory played an important role in the construction of their love. Each time she searched for it, just as she was about to lay hands on a form, the form would disappear and be replaced by another, which wasn't the right one either. He reminded her of a character in a book; of the atmosphere of certain books even. He may also have reminded her of a language; the language of an author she had loved, for example. She leafed through her imagination and recollections, turning over images of characters, but none of them was a perfect fit. With none of them, were he to be laid on top, did he overlap exactly. Perhaps he was a patchwork composed of different images of characters who had moved her.

Summer was drawing to a close, and Thomas Lenz, whom she had kept firmly at arm's length since those first meetings, departed. He was present in her mind all right, but she would shoo him away out of loyalty to Guillaume. It was less than a month later, however, in September, when she was on her own in Paris for a few days for a meeting with the editor of an art magazine and, after lunching with him at the Porte d'Auteuil, felt like a walk in the drizzling rain as the leaves fell in gentle spirals from the trees, that she suddenly said to herself, as if this was what had really been going on inside her since summer, as if she'd at last found the object she had been seeking since summer: But I love him. Yes, that's it, I love him. And as her sister, whom she was staying with, lived on the south side of town in the fourteenth arrondissement, she ended up crossing nearly the whole of Paris on foot in the light mist and the softly falling rain, wearing her new black boots, saying to herself the whole way: But I love him, I love him.

So she looked for a way of communicating with him, if only in her dreams. She didn't want to reach him so much as to satisfy herself it was possible. He lived near the park in Bordeaux—he had mentioned this at some point, and she had made a mental note of it. She checked the internet and the phone book, but there was no trace of him, no postal address or phone number, and on Google only articles he had published or conferences he had attended. There was a photograph of him, however, which she pored over a hundred times. Yes, it was him all right, exactly as she had loved him. Once again, chance came to her aid. At the end of September, while she was at home in Sorge with Guillaume, the magazine she worked for announced that it would be sending her to Bordeaux to review an exhibition there. It was then that she began to feel torn; then that a deep, tragic split began to open in her, like a tear in a long silk dress. Would she try to contact him? Or not bother? She had a cousin in Bordeaux who knew Thomas Lenz's mother vaguely. Would she try to get his phone number from her cousin? She found it in the end and felt relieved. She didn't phone him.

In November, she went down to Bordeaux, and for the two days she was there hoped to run into him in the town center, where she knew he worked and where she would spend the lunch hour strolling back and forth outside dozens of cafés and brasseries. After six, she walked twice round the park, then a third time, and on the second evening crisscrossed the network of streets adjacent to the park. She would have liked him to pop up all of a sudden, walking toward her, as he had in Sorge and then later in the countryside. He didn't. On the train home, now that she had his phone number, she sent him an absurd text message: "I'm on my way home from Bordeaux, where I didn't have time to call you to meet for a drink, but I may be back later for work." Now he has my phone number, she thought to herself, now he can call me. He didn't call. "Till next time, then," he replied in a text, adding "Thank you."

With Guillaume life carried on as usual. Only one thing had changed: she felt less desire for him. In every other respect, she loved him and was very happy with him, while Thomas was confined to what she thought of as daydreams. Deep down, however, she was certain she would run into Thomas again the following summer in Sorge, since he came there every year, and that certainty was a foundation. Guillaume suggested going away together the following August. Anna was okay with any other month of the year, but not August. "Well, that's new," he said, "you always used to say you liked getting away from Sorge in the summer." "I did?" she said. "People change." And she pretended to attach no importance to it all. She was busy with her articles, exhibitions she had to see. Whenever she went to Lille, Lyon, Geneva, Marseilles, she would regret it wasn't Bordeaux. But even in Marseilles or Lausanne she hoped to run into Thomas in the street. After all, she thought, he can travel about, too. From this point on, then, the world was filled with his presence, since anywhere, at any moment, he might appear on a street (it was always a street) and walk toward her.

In March, she had to return to Bordeaux for her work. She had so much to do there that she couldn't look for Thomas, though she did still hope to run into him. In a shop window she saw a dress she was very taken with but didn't have time to try on. Back home in Sorge, the dress took on a life of its own. She wanted it, she had to have it; with that dress, she felt, something would be possible. In May, she announced to Guillaume, who was a bit taken aback but used to Anna's occasional whims, that she wanted to return to Bordeaux to buy this fascinating dress she'd seen in a shop window, the "dress of her life." In reality, he was apprehensive. He wondered what was going on in Bordeaux. But since Anna had become friends with a small group of people connected to the exhibitions, including a certain Odette who phoned her a lot, he felt reassured. She's bored in Sorge, he told himself. She needs to travel about more. In June, therefore, he took her for a fortnight to a beautiful region where they went from village to village, spending a day and a night in the most delightful locations. As always, she felt marvelous with him, they were a perfect match, it would have been unthinkable that another man should pop up; she was just a little less keen on making love, but, sensing that he was alarmed by this, indulged him because she loved him and wanted him to be happy; and besides, she always felt she was growing young again under his caresses.

In May, then, she had returned to Bordeaux to try on the dress she was so taken with and, in all likelihood, buy it. But nothing went off as planned. The Hôtel L'Evêque in the Allées de Tourny, where she had stayed on her previous visits and felt very happy, was full. She wound up in a different hotel, where all that was available was a tiny and rather expensive room under the eaves. In the wardrobe mirror she looked frumpy, with a dress that was too short and a cardigan that didn't go with it at all. Her desire to return to Bordeaux had made her so tense, moreover, that she felt a bit drained. If she went out, she risked bumping into Odette or Cyrille, people connected to the exhibition, who would ask her what she was doing in Bordeaux. Once again she'd have to lie and invent things, for Anna, she now realized, had often found herself in situations where she had had to lie and invent things—she couldn't remember when or where exactly, but still, it felt like she was repeating herself.

She went out to find a brasserie for a light supper, but felt apprehensive, hugging the walls and looking away whenever a car drove by. It was idiotic and out of all proportion: had she run into Cyrille or Odette, it wouldn't have been that hard to say, I have a date. But the date in question was nothing of the sort, it was a most peculiar tryst, more like a meeting with chance or fate than with a man, and for that reason, no doubt, she felt uneasy, even scared perhaps. Never before in her rather settled existence had she undertaken to roam the streets in search of a man she loved. She thought of Adèle H, and of how sure she was of being loved by Lieutenant Pinson, a faith so total that no statement to the contrary, no clear and painstaking explanation on someone else's part, could shake it. Had Anna ever asked herself if Thomas was as lovestruck as she was? No. She was sure of it.

Thomas was indeed, as we shall find out later, waiting. Inside him forms were moving about, indistinct. A mild unease and a glimmer of hope that seemed idle and unreasonable to a man who led a quiet, dispassionate existence and had been expecting to do so to the very end, surprised him, a bit like the first symptoms of an illness, when your body has an unfamiliar ring to it and contracts at an unknown spot, when it's not quite your body any longer, the one you know by heart, but someone else's almost. And he did, in fact, fall ill. Nothing too serious, but something for which light surgery was nevertheless required and as a result of which his sex grew lifeless. He'd been single for some time now, but had no great wish to find a new partner and quite enjoyed being on his own. It was then that he saw Anna in Bordeaux. It was in May, while he was recovering from his operation and having slight difficulties walking. He saw her on the other side of the avenue, hurrying along, for a second he thought of waving to her but didn't—he was furious. She was in Bordeaux and hadn't called him? To hell with her, he thought. And his fury astonished him.

THE DAY AFTER HER arrival in Bordeaux that May, after a rather gloomy supper in an unpleasant brasserie where she hadn't dared order more than a single glass of wine, and then walking back to the hotel in the rain and phoning Guillaume to put his mind at rest, Anna was preparing to make an early start, her batteries replenished and in the frame of mind of someone with a busy day ahead. In reality, she had absolutely nothing to do apart from find the dress she'd already begun to lose interest in and then stroll around town until she ran into Thomas. To pass the time, she popped into a few boutiques, but didn't stay in any for very long for fear it was precisely at that moment Thomas would be coming down the street. She had to be sure she could be seen. She found the boutique with the dress, the dress was still there but wasn't all that special. She tried it on, decided it only half suited her and didn't buy it. In Bordeaux, where she walked for miles that day, she felt as if she were playing that game where one person hides an object and the other hunts for it while you tell them: cold, warm, burning hot, ice cold! In certain streets, and at certain points in the day, it was ice cold and, every now and then, warm, so she would try to go in the direction where it was heating up. At one moment it was hot, then very hot, then burning. But she didn't see him.

In the evening, she passed in front of a handsome building with a handwritten poster on it inviting people to come inside and attend a music class, so she pushed open the door, clambered up a wide staircase and found herself in a large room where ten or so "senior citizens" were holding their hands up like children in response to a zealous schoolmistress, who was questioning them about pieces of music she was playing. She stayed. To end up in a place like this at her age, with her life and plans and energy, was a bit of a fiasco, but she'd often found herself in precisely this kind of situation, if only for an hour or two, once or twice a year. She knew that gap in the soul and the peculiar comfort afforded by these forays into a simpleminded and somewhat pitiful world, a world where she felt completely out of place and almost alarming to the other people present, but where she also knew she could relax for a few minutes. People looked warmly at her and, during the break, stopped just short of offering her one of the cakes the pupils had made; but when the schoolmistress wanted her to sing, she declined and slipped out. Back on the street she felt better; all things considered, it was livelier out than in.

The next morning she felt almost angered that Thomas had failed to appear, so she turned her back on him and went to visit a château on the outskirts of Bordeaux, where at no point did she hope or expect to meet him. In the château, a group of Russians being shown around by a vociferous tour guide walked ahead of her from room to room. She went for a short stroll in the gardens, but was unable to interest herself in anything, being entirely taken up by a faint, quivering rage. She called Guillaume, a little too often probably, since it wasn't like her to be glued to the phone in that way, to tell him that she'd be back the following day as planned, that the dress was ghastly, that she had made a mistake, and then invented an exhibition to explain why she wouldn't be back before nightfall. Guillaume was relieved to hear her sounding so glum.

She knew the following day that she wouldn't see Thomas and that the moment had passed. How can we be so certain of these things? Because our own craving is less pronounced? Less intense? Just to be sure, like someone who's meticulous about her work, she carried on strolling around, veering off from street to street and from square to avenue before stopping for a drink on a café terrace, where a curious scene unfolded: passing in front of a newsstand, a young man snatched up a few magazines and ran off. "Thief! Thief!" cried the newsdealer, whereupon four men rushed off from the terrace in pursuit. She felt like she was in a Vittorio De Sica film, hoping they wouldn't catch the young man as bystanders commented at length on the theft. Opposite her was a palatial white building (the theater?), and overhead, the flowering branches of trees. It was over for now, she knew she wouldn't see him this time round. It soothed her, put her mind at rest. She had done what she had to do, what her whole being had instructed her to do. No one could accuse her of being fainthearted or failing to embrace her destiny. Had she run into him this time, it would have been too easy perhaps, too quick. Affairs of the heart, especially ones like this, are like books; they ask to be written, you can't always find a way in straight off, you have to return to them, persevere, circle round, revise. It's hard work. In a junk shop she bought a pair of tortoiseshell earrings which she never got around to wearing, since she never wore earrings. But making her modest contribution in a little shop in Bordeaux was like tossing a coin into a fountain: a pledge, they say, that you'll be back.

She forgot about him, knowing that it would soon be summer. There was only June and July, then in August she would run into him in Sorge; if not this year, then the next. It was then that Guillaume did something unfortunate. Without mentioning it to her, he had bought an apartment by the sea. He took her to see it as if he had a little surprise in store for her, as if about to announce that the apartment was for the two of them; but when they arrived, she realized he'd been looking to make an investment and would be renting it out instead. It was for their benefit, of course, it would make life more comfortable for them, yet, inexplicably, she felt even more torn, exactly as she had when, armed with Thomas's phone number, she had dallied with him for all that time: Shall I call him? Or shall I not? So powerful, in fact, were the feelings aroused in her by the incident with the apartment that she could have sworn she heard a long split tearing in the silk. But why? She had never wanted an apartment by the sea, and wasn't even all that fond of the sea. Perhaps it was because she had suddenly noticed, for the first time in twenty years—proof of a sort of blindness on her part, a naivety abnormal in someone of her age—that Guillaume wasn't bound only to her, body and soul, but had ideas and plans of his own; which was only natural, she told herself, but it was as if she were being torn from a dream.

She quickly pulled herself together, finding the apartment pleasant and well-situated. It was horribly hot that day, without a breath of wind, and she was waiting for him in the car while he signed the documents with the realtor. He had left the air conditioner on, for he was always making sure she was comfortable and had everything she needed to be happy. Was it then that she had stopped loving him? In that street, in that rather unseemly seaside resort, in the sweltering heat, simply because she had suddenly understood, for the first time in her life, that a man and a woman are separate, that they are never wholly one, as she had so foolishly believed for all those years? And yet it was because she had believed it, and because nothing in her life until then had proved that belief unfounded—or such events, at least, as must certainly have occurred had gone unnoticed by her because of the sheer force of her belief—that she had been so happy with him for so long. It is only by mistake perhaps that we love at all. Not that we mistake the person: Guillaume was better suited to her than anyone she had ever known, and the self-evident nature of their relationship unsettled even young children, who would stop at the sight of them when they weren't even arm in arm or holding hands and yell: "Oooh, the lovebirds!" But she had always believed that Guillaume was bound to her as she was to him, and only now did she understand that a particle of his body and his soul—tiny, no doubt, but real just the same—was unattached to her.

Yes, everything went downhill from that point on, and she would berate herself for not being happier with Guillaume. For the first time, she thought to herself, he has slipped up in the infinitely subtle high-wire act of love, at which he has always excelled. I love him so much, I'm so happy with him, that I shouldn't hold it against him. She didn't hold it against him, however. It was worse than that. It was simply that the tear in the dress had grown, and that there was nothing either of them could do about it. But why has he messed up now, when he's never messed up before? she asked herself, watching him from the edge of the pool at the guesthouse he had brought her to, some twelve miles from the seaside resort. It was a magnificent pool, carved out of stone like a fountain or a *lavoir*. It jutted out over the landscape, and swimming in it was like swimming in the air. They had the house pretty much to themselves, with a garden, a terrace where they could dine alone; they had records and books. She wasn't thinking at all about the other man. Had Thomas popped into her mind just then, she would have thought him much less important than Guillaume. He would have been no match for the grand romance that had bound her to Guillaume for all those years.

The speed with which people can change levels in your consciousness is astonishing. For the next ten months, Guillaume and Thomas shifted back and forth in her mental theater. Sometimes Guillaume was downstage while Thomas was at the rear; at other times, Thomas would appear and Guillaume disappear, and it was like this every day, every hour, every minute sometimes, so that whenever she peered inside herself—and she never did anything else, in thrall to this fascinating play—what she saw there was always new and always uncertain. For a long time she didn't know which of the two she loved, which one she preferred. This one? That one? Both? Neither? They were like the two sides of a coin. Should she toss the coin to decide, heads or tails? She tossed the coin, it was heads; she tossed the coin a second time, it was tails.

Then, unfortunately, summer arrived. It was beautiful in Sorge and scorching hot, but the temperature cooled at night, so you could sleep peacefully and sit out in the evening, relieved to have to put on a sweater or a shawl. Again she felt very happy with Guillaume; she was waiting for Thomas. Since she knew where his house was, she had driven past it once or twice. Then one day she noticed that the shutters were open and was overcome with joy. Tomorrow, she said to herself, tomorrow you'll be in Sorge, at the same spot at the same hour, I'll leave the house, slightly behind time to see if you're prepared to wait for me, but I'll run into you. So off she went the next morning, confident, a quarter of an hour late: he was there at the same spot, chatting with a man he knew, in plain sight, right in the middle of the street. Startled, she dashed into a pharmacy, bought a toothbrush, recovered her composure, and, as she walked up to him, felt an extravagant smile playing about her face, a smile that had never been hers and which was meant to be amicable and welcoming, but for all that was not her usual smile.

They chatted as though nothing untoward was happening, but, in the meantime, Anna's sister had turned up and greeted him, so he proposed that the three of them dine together the following evening in a restaurant he liked in the countryside. Guillaume was away for eight days. Laure was fine with the proposal, Anna accepted, and they agreed to meet at his house the following day and go on from there in his car. The next day, it was Laure who took the wheel for the drive to Thomas's. In the car something extraordinary happened: after a moment, Anna, who hardly ever wept, burst into tears. Laure was taken aback and, alarmed, pulled over and asked Anna if there had been bad news (Guillaume had called her on her cellphone a few minutes earlier). Anna feigned fatigue, a moment of depression, for she herself had no idea what was happening. The truth was that she was in the process of joining Thomas and leaving Guillaume, that her life was breaking up, there beneath the trees on a road through a wood, their twenty years of life together, a life that had been so happy, and in exchange there was this blurred image that refused to be coupled with any existing image yet never ceased to recall one. The split widened a notch.

She was afraid of looking ghastly after crying so much, so Laure made a detour into the neighboring village, where a fairground had been set up. They got out, wandered among the booths and chatted with some people they knew; little by little Anna settled down, Laure sensed this, and they arrived at Thomas's house at last, where, at the sound of the car in his driveway, he appeared on the doorstep. My God, it was his home! He showed them around. There wasn't a single object, a single shape, color, or instant, that escaped Anna's attention. It was like focusing very hard on a book. The house, she was relieved to find, was rather gloomy. Then Thomas drove them to the restaurant he liked in the depths of the countryside. Laure had insisted Anna sit up front, so Thomas was on Anna's left, driving. Caught in the headlights all of a sudden, they saw a fox, stock-still in the middle of the road. Thomas stopped, the fox's heart must have been beating so hard it would break, the scene lasted a few seconds. Then, after weighing the risk of being killed against the odds of surviving, and as if staking his all, the fox slowly crossed the road, only bounding into the meadow once he had reached the verge.

In the restaurant, Thomas didn't flirt with her at all, he didn't so much as glance at her even, but their love was already at its height. Since he was beside her, with Laure seated opposite, Anna could smell the rather bleak, acrid scent of his body; she disliked it, and, as invariably happens at the start of a love story of this kind, felt hugely relieved that she didn't like the smell, and therefore didn't love him. When they left the restaurant, they stood for a long time gazing out over a deep valley and its lights, all three of them smoking in the keen, bracing air. She was no longer so sure she hadn't liked the smell. She vaguely told herself she would have to give it another try, just to be sure.

Did she feel she was cheating on Guillaume? Of course she did. But it was as if a certain back-and-forth between her life and her dreams was no longer possible. She had no thoughts for the future, and it simply didn't occur to her that she might one day have to leave Guillaume, regardless of how things turned out. Nor did she dream of having an affair with Thomas. She would have liked to have both men, if they might share out the hours in her: one for daytime and sun, the other for nighttime and sleep. And without grasping what this meant, she thought it would be possible.

LATER, WHEN SHE WOULD think back on that day and on the many that were to follow, Anna would be astounded by the force of the passion that had taken hold of her. Not that a passion of that kind was unknown to her. It had happened twice before in her life, and in the same manner. It was as though some dark corner of yourself had suddenly burst into flame, and all the more violently for having been soaked in petrol or alcohol beforehand. The flames shot straight into the air, licking and blackening the walls and burning the house down, as the gigantic shapes and shadows they traced danced a mesmerizing jig. The two previous experiences, however, had been unhappy; neither man had wanted anything to do with this woman and her outlandish, burning passion. After the first few months of rapturous joy, she had found herself in a state of despair at failing to attain the loved one's body, and her suffering had been every bit as acute as previously her desire had been. Life doesn't teach us much, it seems, for here she was, starting all over again. The trouble is that the suffering we forget, while the memory of joy remains keen. Someone only has to stir that memory and we immediately want to be overcome with the desire we mistake for love, and which can sometimes become love, but which in reality is nothing more than an irrepressible longing to lie naked beside someone.

But this time something had changed. On the two previous occasions when she had conceived a burning passion for someone, she'd never been quite sure the other party would respond; she'd probably even known from the outset he wouldn't. In Thomas she had glimpsed the possibility, not only of a response, but of a fire identical to her own. How had she seen this? Who knows . . . ? Each morning (or every other morning sometimes, for they needed to catch their breath and rest a bit, no doubt), they would run into each other in Sorge, and sometimes in another part of town, for there was no need any longer to focus on the precise spot where they'd first met. Fate, having slipped into gear, was easing up. Anna would go out, pick up a couple of items of shopping and then stroll about, going as far as the café terrace facing the countryside or the town hall opposite. Thomas, meanwhile, would have gone to see a mechanic on the outskirts of town or to visit a friend, but it was most unusual if, some time around eleven, he didn't pop up all of a sudden, even in some obscure side street, walking toward her. Without remarking on their chance encounter, they would have a coffee somewhere and talk about the town, their activities, what they were reading, but never of personal matters, and never face to face, seated together, side by side, at the small round bistro table.

Why didn't they come straight to the point? To begin with, because hovering around each other in this way was delightful, and Thomas in any case was a little wary of Anna, finding it hard to understand what was going on in her head; but also because, standing between them—in Anna's brain, her flesh, her life, in all her thoughts and emotions—was Guillaume. Thomas again invited her to dinner, but on her own this time, and then to go for a walk together, but each time she declined. He deduced from this that it was friendship she wanted, but everything about her was so at odds with the idea of a friendship that he thought he must have some sort of seductress or Jezebel on his hands. It was at this point that she mentioned her relationship with Guillaume. He felt disappointed and annoyed, decided he would treat this peculiar woman as a pleasant holiday acquaintance, and spent the next few days visiting the region, only returning to Sorge in the late afternoon.

A week went by without their meeting, and each morning Anna would regret not running into him. In the meantime, Guillaume had returned, and, since he often had the afternoon off, they would go swimming in a lake they'd discovered in the early days of their love, a lake they had all to themselves and which played an important part in their story. They would make their way down through a meadow holding each other firmly by the hand; she loved him. They'd find their way back to the little creek, where he would carefully tamp down the earth so that she could stretch out comfortably, and then lie there together staring into space, while above them flickering pine branches seemed tinseled with gold and silver like the branches of a Christmas tree. They would make love with the force and familiarity of old lovers, swim naked (since visitors seldom came near the lake), chase each other, laughing, through the cold, metallic water, cuddle some more and discover stones or fish they had never seen before. Above them the sky was bright blue, Guillaume was happy, and Anna was happy, too. Thomas was a tiny blip on her radar, an extravagance of summer. By the end of August, he'd be gone. There was no point alarming Guillaume, it would only cause him pain.

The mornings, however, were hard. Then, on the

eve of his departure, Thomas reappeared. They had coffee together and talked about books; back in Bordeaux he happened to have a rare book that she was looking for, and he asked her for her address so that he could send it to her. Then it was the day of his departure, and suddenly Sorge and the surrounding countryside were empty; so empty, in fact, that it was as if she had fallen into a sort of black hole and was tumbling and spinning around in it. Later that afternoon there was to be a gathering of Guillaume's family, with parents and children and grandchildren. After lunch, she went swimming in a different lake, one she usually enjoyed, where bathers and anglers were constantly warring with each other, where the banks were covered with thick grass and the tall trees ideal for not getting sunburned, where you would often run into friends, and where the view as you swam in the warm silk pursued by tiny swift tree frogs was magnificent. Her anguish was at its height. It was a long time since she'd felt that way, a very long time. She tried reading an old novel she couldn't interest herself in and almost drowned a small child some friends had entrusted her with while they went swimming in another part of the lake.

Among Guillaume's family—at a beautiful house with a large garden where some twenty or so guests were chatting about the summer and their vacations—she felt horribly alone, though everyone was very nice to her. She had a pretty dress on and regretted that Thomas wasn't there to see it. She imagined him on the road to Bordeaux, stony-faced and secretive behind the windshield as he smoked and listened to music. She wondered if he was thinking about her, or if he had other matters on his mind, other plans and preoccupations. She would have liked him to send her a text message that evening, telling her he'd arrived home safely. Oh for heaven's sake, she was crazy. He wasn't her lover, he wasn't her partner. And Guillaume felt uneasy, because this woman he knew by heart, and who if anything was lively and gay, always lively and gay, looked strange to him. It must be a hormonal thing, he told himself.

She still hadn't understood, then, that Thomas was a real human being. She still believed, and had for a year now, that this figure who kept popping up and whom she found so striking was a fictional character, someone to be looked for in a book or in the recollection of a book, whereas he was simply a man, with his life, his failings, his sufferings, his joys, his satisfactions. It must be strange to be mistaken for somebody else like that. Rather unpleasant perhaps. Anna had once sparked a passion of this kind in a young Danish artist. The young man, who had been staying in Sorge with his wife and had been invited over by Guillaume and her on several occasions, since they found them charming, was besotted with Anna, whom he could no longer see as anything but a figure in a painting. He was crazy about her, which she found odd. Whenever she spent any time with him, she would treat him as a nurse would a patient: gently, delicately, but rather taken aback by his folly. At roughly the same period, she had gone to visit an old friend in Rome for a few days, and this crackpot, George, had followed her there, like a character in a novel or a poem by an eighteenth-century German Romantic. It was rather flattering, no doubt, to be the object of an illusion like this (not everyone can be the object of an illusion), but above all it was odd. It was as if she had to glance behind her all the time to see who it was he really loved; as though standing silently behind her was the beloved woman conjured up by her presence. The episode ended badly: he abandoned his wife and child to live in a fervent, tormented solitude. Later on came a string of young women all of whom resembled Anna, just as Anna resembled a figure in a painting that he longed to merge with.

Thomas had initially reminded her of Jude the Obscure. And also of Hardy himself, since Thomas's house near Sorge resembled the other Thomas's house, which she had visited one day on a trip to Dorset. It's quite possible that, in reality, the two houses weren't at all alike, for Anna often noticed similarities between things where none existed. There'd been a time when she had loved *Jude the Obscure,* which was thoroughly confused in her mind with Samuel Butler's *The Way of All Flesh.* Guillaume, on the other hand, had never reminded her of a character in a book. Guillaume was Guillaume, she had never felt a need to look beyond or behind him. His presence was clear, steady, monumental. He couldn't be distilled into ten different images like playing cards, she didn't have to shuffle them about as she did with Thomas, changing their positions and turning them over as if her own fate were at stake. In addition to Jude, Thomas reminded her in varying degrees of a dozen other characters: some of these she could name, while for others, all she could recall were silhouettes that she couldn't assign a name or a precise identity to; for others still, it was just a type of character or presence in this or that book, and occasionally in a film.

In any event—and she felt ridiculous saying this one day—he was the one she "had always been waiting for." Very early on, as young as ten perhaps—or perhaps even six, who knows?—an image had formed in her mind of a man representing love. What had so shocked her the first time she set eyes on Thomas was his resemblance to that figure. To tell the truth, it was the first time she had seen embodied in the flesh an image she had always had in her mind, but would have been quite incapable of describing, since it didn't have the precision of a photo; yet when she saw Thomas he fitted that image exactly. What was strange was that she must have run into him on other occasions, in previous years, since he often spent his holidays in Sorge. Perhaps at the time she'd had eyes for nothing else, her field of consciousness being wholly taken up by Guillaume and her love for him. Blessed era, when a quiet, happy life was still possible.

When you meet someone who reminds you powerfully of someone else but you don't know who, the sensible thing to do, no doubt, is to run for your life. What prevents you from doing so, alas, like a pact with the devil, is the promise of bliss that the apparition holds out. But even bliss, perhaps, is best avoided: it's probably not an acceptable state for mankind. Alas, the whole world urges you to merge with that image, imagining it to be ideal. Hopelessly in love in this way, Anna felt a need to confide in others, to gather together their views and thoughts on the matter, and, in so doing, to furnish herself with handrails perhaps. She had to go up to Paris a lot that year for work. She would meet with each of her friends in turn, some eight or ten of them in all, most of whom she had been close to since her student days. Every time one of them asked, "How are you?", she would tell the story. The men would urge caution; the women would marvel at her good fortune and vitality: falling head over heels in love again at her age, how lucky she was! Anna would emphasize the tragic side of the situation: Guillaume, her love for Guillaume and his for her. Often as not, the men would side with Guillaume, the women with the unbridled passion.

She was so lost that she even poured her heart out to her gynecologist and her hairdresser, as well as to an elderly couple who had been friends with her grandparents. Everyone, she said to herself, knows something about love; by listening to their views, I'll figure out what to do. The gynecologist was against the whole thing, the elderly couple were at a loss. At the hairdresser's, on the other hand, the moment she told one of the stylists about her romance she found herself surrounded at the next appointment by three marveling, questioning faces: "And then what?" "And then," she went on, "I wavered, I hesitated, I didn't know what to do." All were on the side of love, all three thought it marvelous to dare to turn your life around, they saw so many customers grumpy and depressed at having wasted their lives. Whereas here they were with Anna—inspired, elated, and tormented too, of course, but on behalf of such a noble cause. She must, she simply *had to* embrace her fate. They had all experienced powerful attractions in the past and had turned their backs on them. It was something they'd always regret, they said. Anna was their advanced guard, she would accomplish what they'd never dared to do. They would feel horribly let down if she threw in the towel. And they took special care of her hair, "for the new man."

Anna by this time was lying to Guillaume, for what she was hiding took up more and more space inside her. The book Thomas had promised to send her had arrived, together with a short note. She pored over his handwriting, which she was seeing for the first time. He had a writer's hand, she thought. She would have to thank him for the book, of course. She wrote back with a short note of her own, but stumbled when it came to signing off. She couldn't write "Love," nor could she put, "See you soon," since there was no question of seeing him again before the following summer. So she wrote "Hugs and kisses," knowing full well that she was opening the floodgates, but believing that she'd still be able to stem the tide. It had the desired effect. He sent her a text message asking her for her email address, at which point she knew that if she gave it to him her previous life was over. She was in Paris down by the Seine when the text message arrived, and about to cross the Pont des Arts. It gave her such a shock that her heart began beating very fast, like the heart of that fox on the country road, torn between the terror of dying and a violent wish to survive. She crossed the Pont des Arts, walked through the Cour Carrée at the Louvre, circumnavigated the Pyramid, went back through the Cour Carrée and back across the bridge, and then started over again. This went on for two hours, at the end of which she sent a cautious, "I'd rather we let a little time pass first." Feeling relieved, she was making her way back up the rue de Seine when he replied: "Another ten years?" Six days later, she phoned him.

NOT TO FLING HERSELF into his arms, no, certainly not. Just to give him that address, which it would have been ridiculous to refuse. They would send each other emails, chatting as they had done over coffee back in Sorge. It was of no real importance. She just needed to be in touch with him, to talk to him, that was all. She didn't say anything to Guillaume, who wouldn't have understood, wouldn't have approved, would have fretted about it. How foolish men are, she said to herself, to fret about something as natural as the need to be in touch with someone. Guillaume sensed she had changed, though he couldn't have said how or why. There was something different about the way she looked at him, he thought. "Don't be silly," she said, tired of his suspicions and his demonstrations of love, which had suddenly become awkward and out of place, untimely—he, who had always had a gift for adapting to the flow of time, her moods, her imaginative world, the shifting terrain of their life together. "Don't be silly, I'm just a bit tired, I need more time to myself to work." And the anguish she could feel peeping through in Guillaume tormented and pained her. If only he would let her run wild and not worry about it, if only he'd just go on being happy with her because he loved her the way she was, it would have made her so happy.

Instead, it was their emails that ran amok, as Thomas became her great morning magic. A poor sleeper, he would rise early and send her an email to say hello, together with a few lines describing what he was up to that day. Around nine, when Guillaume had gone off to work, she would read the email and reply. She, too, spoke about her life and what she was doing that day. After a while, Thomas began to feel unwell. He was getting less and less sleep, felt flustered and couldn't understand why. She, too, was sleeping badly and felt flustered, but knew exactly why. He was running a fever; so was she. He was having difficulties working, concentrating; so was she. Their symptoms' similarities astonished them. Was he faking his? Perhaps not. He was disconcerted by this woman who kept saying "I want you" and "I don't want you." There was something else, though, something even more peculiar: she had awakened a memory in him. A memory long buried, long concealed, very ancient, the memory of something tragic in his childhood. Upon contact with Anna during their coffees together in Sorge, this very ancient thing which he thought had been laid to rest forever had stirred. And what was odd, what was terrifying almost, was that it was as if Anna when speaking to him was addressing that child. Not the powerful man in him, with a distinguished profession, delightful children from the time of his marriage, and a whole life behind him. No, that wasn't the one she was addressing, nor was it the one she was attracted to, the one she was fascinated by. It was the other one, the boy seized by a pain that would never pass. That was why, though he didn't have the words for it yet, he was crazy about her.

At the time, she knew nothing of all this. But what she found so attractive in him was, yes, a wound, what else could she call it, a wound that was the exact—no, the *ideal*—counterpart to her own. Guillaume had certainly had to deal with that wound, but as a doctor, not as a brother in poverty. Guillaume was strong, radiant, workmanlike, very gentle, with a gift for healing. When he had encountered Anna and her wound, he had tended it over and over again, beautifully, lovingly, through each of his acts and deeds, without fussing over it, treating her harshly at times, forcing her to assume responsibilities she would have thought herself quite incapable of assuming, goading her on, having her climb summits when she couldn't possibly, she'd protest, go a step further, poking fun at her, supporting her, wrapping her in his arms and never taking his eyes off her for a second. Guillaume had cared for her like no one in the world had ever cared for her. But unfortunately for Guillaume, she had met Thomas, the other side of the coin; Thomas who, like her, had made the most of his existence, founding his strength on his wound and leading a life that, while not overly cheerful, was dignified, interesting, and strong, with its moments of joy. And in a glance—how is such a thing possible with just a glance?—Anna and he had recognized each other.

Yes, during that first coffee in the summer of 2002, at a time when they knew nothing about each other or their respective lives, she had been struck by something. While talking about her article, he had mentioned being particularly touched by a passage in which she had described unbridled passion. He kept coming back to it, saying he had known that, had experienced those emotions. And she had sensed that he was talking about something else, something greater almost than love. Not about his boyhood passion for a young girl; not about his youthful passion for a young woman. No, in reality he was alluding to something he might not even have been aware of, a very powerful childhood emotion, a violation of his sensibility. Seated all around them at the café tables were people chatting, some of whom she knew by sight or had exchanged a few words with in the past. She knew full well that it was a perfectly ordinary morning, yet when she looked up, the square where they were seated, and which she had known since time immemorial, had changed.

Had she had a mother to confide in at this point, the latter would certainly have urged caution, she might even have succeeded in keeping her in check. But she didn't have that card in her deck. Guillaume himself would later say: but why didn't you mention it to me at the time? But in this matter Guillaume was probably not the ideal interlocutor, and there are things, moreover, which have to remain secret. Secrecy is the dross they are mixed with. It's their mother tongue, in fact. You can pretend to disclose them to your hairdresser or your gynecologist, to certain friends, but in reality you disclose nothing, you just appear to be talking about a love affair, an awkward choice to be made between two men, and by transforming your story into that of millions of men and women since the world began—falling in love with someone when you're perfectly happy with someone else—laying bare a very ancient conflict to which no one has ever found a solution. "You have to choose," said some, "you have to decide one way or the other." "You should conduct the affair in secret but stay with Guillaume," said others. "You have to let it go," urged some. "But you must know which one you truly love," declared still others. But how can you choose in life without cutting your own self in two? For it's not about, on the one hand, a man, and on the other, another. It's about a life—beating, quivering like an organ laid bare—to which both men belong; and if you break with one of them, whichever one it might be, you might not survive.

Was it then that she thought for the first time of taking her own life? No, surely not, the idea only crossed her mind much later when things got seriously out of hand. There was a long tradition of suicide in Anna's family: at exactly her age, first her mother, and then one of her sisters had decided to depart this life. In her mother's case, Anna had never quite understood what had possessed her. In the case of her sister, there was manifestly an obstacle standing in her way that made living quite impossible for her, an impediment so great that it prevented her not only from being happy, but even from drawing breath. On each occasion when the fire of life had been extinguished in one of these women, Anna had valiantly taken up the flame; and besides, with Guillaume she was safe, no harm could ever befall her, so full and rich and happy was their life together.

They would go on the most incredible walks, walks she knew only too well she would never go on with Thomas. Guillaume loved walking and clambering about and was continually whisking her off to some summit somewhere. His addiction to hiking was almost comical. Ophidian by nature, she would have preferred to remain behind in a garden or a bedroom, reading, smoking, sniffing flowers, watching an insect going about its life, rubbing a pebble between her fingers, and listening to church bells ringing in the distance. No, no, he would say. He needed the open air, the physical exertion, he needed to feel his body, and perhaps more than anything, to push his way along some rugged mule track to a mountain plateau where the view was always a triumph.

In the early days, she would tag along, grumbling a bit to please him, but in no time at all, from the moment of their very first hikes together, beneath a leaden sky in the Ardèche or in the mist and rain of the Pyrenees, and sometimes during the very first hour of their ascent, an extraordinary joy and peace would come over her. Within a few years, she had grown so fond of these excursions that her eyes would light up, her body spring to attention, at the prospect of a vacation approaching when they would set out with their boots and walking sticks, passing through villages she would never have dared pass through alone, along paths she would never even have noticed. Though relatively inexperienced, she never felt tired. He would laugh at the sight of her scrambling about like a goat and never once feeling dizzy, or sitting down for a second on the edge of a precipice as though it was the safest and most comfortable spot in the world. They ate melon and tomatoes and salami. He was always the one with the knapsack across his shoulders, he would never let her burden herself with anything. They walked through waterfalls, swam in icy water, saw animals leap out in front of them, lost their way, found new paths, and never met a soul, entirely alone with each other.

After a while, these enchanted and enchanting hikes, from which they'd come back exhausted but ready to start all over again the next day, came to play an increasingly prominent role in their life. It was as if the center of their love had shifted. Not that they didn't have other joys, other pleasures, in the world below, it was simply that the joy of dining together on a village square, of sharing a new house far from home and exploring a new region, even of kissing and cuddling in bed at night, would lose in intensity what it gained on the heights. Perhaps that was why they had to start all over again each time, since Anna was never closer to Guillaume than when they were on these mountain paths together. As for Guillaume, you can't help wondering why he led her up there so often. Was he afraid her love for him would melt away in the world below? He would sometimes say with a laugh that the lengths he had to go to to keep her entertained, to arouse her curiosity and enthusiasm, were colossal. He loved to see her happy and carefree, singing to herself like a child. And yet it was only in the mountains now that she was like this. In the world below, she would often be hurting somewhere; in her belly, her back, her head, there would be a small pain shifting about, pausing here or there, making her grumpy, little disposed to love, and uneasy about she didn't know what exactly.

The moment they made their way up a village street, climbing above the rooftops and in the blink of an eye leaving them far below, the moment they pushed into open country not visible from the road, where all they could smell was the odor of their heated bodies sweating from exertion mixed with the scent of grass and scree, Anna's heart, it seemed, grew lighter. She would start smiling and chattering like a magpie, crying out, caressing the silky tissue of a plant or a tuft of grass, while her gaze trained firmly on the summit seemed armed for the fight. Sometimes she would stride on ahead of him, increasingly less tired the higher she climbed, leaving the affairs of the world behind her, down below, all the memories that hurt and hold you back, all the complications of furnishing a world she often found empty, all the conversations and relations with others that she was by no means inimical to, but often found wearisome.

Was this the same woman, then, who in Bordeaux had gone back and forth in search of her imagined love, veering off from one street to the next with an intensity and determination that gave her the feeling—certainly mistaken—of being at the center of her true life? What could this goat child bounding along mountain paths possibly have in common with the woman who had executed an interminable series of volts and demivolts in Bordeaux? The act of walking, no doubt. Anna's legs were slender, firm and muscular, for one of the things she had done a lot of in her life, in addition to smoking, reading, and dreaming, was walking. And with Guillaume, moreover, whether on an ochre dirt track among the pines, in dense scrubland where they had lost their way and had spent a long time searching for the exit as if in a maze, or on a path overlooking an abyss where the ledge was so narrow that you had to think imperatively of anything but the void in order not to fall—she would often sing at the top of her voice the opening bars of *The Soldier's Tale* ("Marching,

marching all the day"), which she'd seen performed in Sorge in her sixteenth year.

They fell ill, then, Thomas and Anna, after that summer in 2003 when they began meeting again. Their emails read like medical reports: "Slept a little better, how about you?" "Toothache, spent the whole afternoon at the dentist's." They didn't dare meet. Anna reread *La Princesse de Clèves* to find out how you resist, how you let go. She still hadn't said anything to Guillaume, for she was determined to stay in love with him, this business with Thomas was decidedly insane. Whenever she thought about it she would picture a rock split in two by an explosion. She would see this fractured, pale-colored rock, under a piercing light and a bright blue sky like the skies painted by Cézanne. There was nothing sinister about the sight: on the contrary, it was as if the stone's heart had been laid bare at last, with its soft, suave interior and its treasury of veins. But all around, the landscape was motionless, silent, perfectly indifferent, as nature always is. It was only normal, she thought, that she should have a slight toothache, a stomachache, a backache, after a jolt like that. But the pain needed to subside, for nothing can be founded, not even a conversation, on a fracture of that kind.

At more settled moments in her life, Anna, each

time some powerful emotion or torment came crashing down, would compare her situation, which was essentially very happy, to that of people who had had to endure some terrible misfortune foisted on them from without. And she would feel ashamed for being so extravagantly affected by little setbacks and misunderstandings, fallings-out. At moments like these she would have been capable of remarking that women given to falling passionately in love are often idle, with nothing much to do with their time and seldom any care for the morrow. Could anyone imagine Phèdre with a job? It's a spiritual luxury, being in a position to enjoy these overwhelming emotions, which can certainly kill you or drive you insane, but at the same time are the mark of some deep-seated transformation. And yet it's so wonderful to have the leisure to be transformed, to give yourself up to this perilous play, when so many people are compelled to think, first and foremost, of simply hanging on.

Yet whenever she was overcome with desire like this at the sight of Thomas, she would lose the ability to compare, to see herself from the outside, and would live exclusively with her powerful emotions, pressed up against them, tucked up inside them, feeling their warmth and life like a cat ensconced in a basket with her litter of newborn kittens. The moment she ran into Thomas she ceased to think; such is the tour de force of passion. She was nothing but a whirling body in the streets of Sorge in summer, desirous not so much of merging her flesh with his as of being pressed up naked against him. As if that contact, the act of reaching and touching his body, would turn her into a tree in leaf, would transform her all of a sudden. She had never wished for this with Guillaume—unless, of course, she had forgotten about it, since everything gets forgotten in the end. Guillaume she had wanted to merge with on the very first day, and how they had galloped about for twenty years! Thomas, on the other hand, she simply wanted to touch; she wanted to press her chest against his, as if a sort of transfusion would then come about; the rest they could see about later. Still, she couldn't help wondering what his sex was like.

SHE WAS CURIOUS ABOUT that sex. She would have liked to know how it was shaped, to look at it and touch it. Basically, she said to herself, I would like to know Thomas intimately, it's his privacy that attracts me. She would have liked to know how this man, who was so secretive and, in a way, so insulated from the world, behaved and what he was like naked, in the act of love. Whenever she saw him in the distance in Sorge, coming toward her, the sight of his high, hard, mute and, as it were, closed silhouette enchanted her. With other men, the sensuality is more apparent, the body is one with its intentions, the possibility of sex is undisguised, and you don't have the impression that in seeing them naked or making love you would discover anything. When she had met Guillaume she had known straightaway he would be a wonderful lover, warm and attentive, greedy and joyous, and when they spent their first night together it was exactly as she'd imagined, with one difference: that making love did wonders for her soul, something she would never have expected from the act of love. But of Thomas nothing could be known, nothing surmised. Other than a surprise, perhaps, something unheard-of.

Could she imagine herself naked with another man? With anyone else, no. With Thomas, yes, for in that case she'd be a different person. She'd have the body of a young girl—slimmer, freer, tighter—the body of a child as yet unvisited. She would ask herself sometimes if she hadn't made love with Guillaume too much, too often, too passionately. Her body was still graceful, but sometimes she felt as if she was a thousand years old, had had seven children, had been penetrated over and over, had been fondled and kissed too much. That body with all its experience weighed on her a bit. With Thomas she'd be a virgin, she'd start afresh, he'd be less invasive inside her than Guillaume had been, he'd leave her freer to be twelve forever. And whenever she daydreamed about his sex or his naked silhouette, in his thick-walled house in Sorge where inevitably, there was no getting round it, she would one day join him, she would think of that encounter as a kind of ballet, spectral but intense, that would leave her inviolate even though he had just made love to her.

In the midst of all the emails they exchange, sometimes several times a day, alluding solely to their strange afflictions (they've both stopped eating and are losing weight), their occupations, their thoughts—she's keen on this long-distance correspondence, for she's not yet done with the *event* of their meeting and would like to carry on strolling through Sorge in her mind—she keeps coming back to his way of appearing on a street, having him pop up and then disappear, then pop up again, as in that game you play with tiny children. Hamlet? Yes, there's a bit of Hamlet about him, or Lorenzaccio perhaps, in his black doublet (does Lorenzaccio really wear a black doublet?), though he also resembles the mysterious watchmaker in the rue Gay-Lussac in Paris who sells hourglasses and water clocks and is himself the spitting image of that famous Russian poet familiar to us from black and white photos. She loves playing with that puppet on her stage, it amuses her no end: he appears, he disappears, he appears, he disappears, and every now and then she has him pop up, as if by surprise, on a street corner where she's never seen him before. It's all she can do not to burst out laughing and start clapping her hands. It would be so marvelous, she thinks to herself, if nothing had the slightest importance, if you could just play like this, like a child plopped down on the rug, in a bedroom, inventing characters, moving shadows back and forth and deciding that here you have a field, here a forest, over here lovers meeting, and down here a threat you ward off just in time with a roadblock, a barrier.

She's playing on the rug in the salon, on the ground floor of Thomas's house near Sorge. Yes, she knows it's a little odd to be playing like this, that she's dragging down in her fall two men who don't have a clue what's going on and want only to love her and be good to her. In her folly she's sowing the seeds of catastrophe. The trouble is that bliss and pain, Guillaume and Thomas, day and night, have struck up a fabulous, frenzied dance inside her. Sometimes it's day you see in the spotlight, sometimes night, sometimes it's Guillaume's back, sometimes Thomas's face; she longs with all her soul to be able to say: "Stop! Stop!" and to sit herself down on a bench, but the moment one of them says, "I'm out of here!" she starts up again, and the moment the other one says, "Enough!" she starts up again, and when she herself decides to put a halt to it all, a few hours later she again feels a need, not to perform this dance, which she finds exhausting and which they all find exhausting, but to reestablish contact, first with one of them, then with the other, and away they all go again. After reflecting for a few minutes on her tale, the elderly couple who had been friends with her grandparents had put their finger on it: "Something dramatic needs to happen," the thoughtful old man had said. "Yes, a bolt from the blue to free you from this quandary," went on the old lady. And just as Anna was about to leave and had parted the portiere covering the door to the apartment, the old lady went back into her salon to fetch something. She returned with a postcard from the Fifties—Anna had not yet been born—on the back of which Anna's mother had sent her greetings, and handed it to her with a look that spoke volumes, as if in provision for the journey.

Whenever she was up in Paris, Anna liked to visit the elderly couple. The large apartment they inhabited was so bright and so peaceful that, the moment you stepped inside, it was as if you had left behind all the burdens of life, all the joys and torments of the world. Still cheerful, still curious, still sprightly, and married now for sixty-eight years, they would question her about her life and occupations, rising from their chairs to jot down on a sheet of paper the title of a book or an exhibition, to find a photo of their latest great-grandchild or, in a cupboard, an embroidered tablecloth they had mentioned during Anna's previous visit and which she had asked to see. Anna wondered what Antoinette, the old lady, would have done in her shoes. Antoinette would have made her choice; she wouldn't have hesitated for more than a week. She would have examined the situation, opted for the solution that seemed best suited to her happiness and peace of mind, put an end to one man's torment and made the other man's day, she would have stood by her decision, consenting to the servitudes and elaborating on the joys: in a word, Antoinette would have pledged herself. Anna, on the other hand, had never pledged herself to anyone and was quite incapable of doing so. She had met Guillaume, their love had proved lasting, and when other men had fallen under her spell she had never been troubled by it; as for the two great unconsummated passions she had experienced before meeting Thomas, one dated from before her time with Guillaume, the other from the middle of their life together, so she'd never had to choose. The only man she had chosen in her life was Guillaume, but with no idea at the time if their love would last one year, ten years, or sixty. Never before had she imagined one could pledge oneself, though the whole world turned on that; as if love for her was simply a form of magic, not this companionship where you also cared for your other half. Guillaume had cared for her well. But had she ever thought of caring for him? She was gentle and affectionate with him, of course; but did she ever really worry about his own worries? But you would have thought he didn't have any, his happiness consisting wholly in watching over Anna.

And yet when this burning desire for Thomas had first declared itself, a strange thought which was quite out of character had crossed Anna's mind: namely, that he was the only man she could imagine herself marrying. It had occurred to her perhaps the second time she saw him. It was an insane idea, which she drove from her mind, a conception of romantic love quite different from her own. With Thomas, she said to herself, she would have someone both to respect and to protect. What she admired in Guillaume was his marvelous vitality, his love of physical exertion, the delight he took in whatever he happened to be doing; but never, not once in twenty years, had it crossed her mind to protect him. Perhaps he himself was overprotective of her? In her daydreams about Thomas she tried to slip into the role of the bride. Sometimes, passing a church, she would go inside and imagine a mystic marriage with Thomas. His figure, it seemed to her, was suited to hers, his carriage to hers, his somewhat dry manner to her passion, his wounded sensibility to hers, his voice to hers, and his body, my God, his body was closer to hers than Guillaume's, which was like Zeus inseminating Leda.

But in this too she was mistaken, of course. It was in her imagination once again that she would see Guillaume as a sort of God the Father, a Jupiter figure, an all-powerful being, whereas the poor fellow was simply a man with his fears, his difficulties, perhaps even his sorrows. His one crime was his radiant presence. When she was beside him, it was like a warm rock she was touching, an oak tree in a bare meadow. It was blissful to be a sort of mortal watched over by this beneficent and all-powerful god, to have this king at your side. There was nothing he couldn't fix. The television in the house they had rented was broken? They needed to drive seven hundred miles in a day? They had lost their way in a mountain fastness at nightfall? She was worried sick because her sister who would later kill herself wanted to die and was going crazy? She couldn't finish an article she was writing? She suddenly felt like a glass of champagne at three o'clock in the morning? She needed a painkiller on a Sunday in the middle of the countryside? She was scared or cold? Whatever it was, he would come to her rescue. He would get the television repaired or find a cinema. He would drive seven hundred miles without flagging, putting on music for her, tipping her seat back so that she could sleep, stopping at a service station to buy her candy. In the mountains, when it was cold and pouring with rain, he would give her his sweater, wrap his anorak around her shoulders and leave her with the cell phone so that she wasn't alone while he went off in his shirt to scout around. When he came back an hour later, he'd not only found the path but had brought her cherries. Anna's sister was insane? He would leave Anna free to do her work, whatever she thought fit, accompanying her wherever she needed to go, waiting for her for eight hours at a stretch sometimes. And when she came back ashen-faced, he would take her off to eat oysters, try to distract her, clasp her tight. She couldn't finish an article? He would poke fun at her, laughing, telling her she was the finest art critic in the world, and then go out for four or five hours so that she could work at her article, though he had nothing to do outside. And when one night, in the countryside near a village called Grignan, Anna's body, once again apprehensive about something, broke out in red blotches and she started to have difficulties breathing, he found heaven knows how a pharmacy open somewhere—he probably forced them to open—and came back with the medication that brought her instant relief.

If she were to fall ill with Thomas, who would care for her? She went to see a psychoanalyst whom she consulted from time to time, explaining her discomfort and distress, her dilemma: on the one hand, she dreamed of returning to Bordeaux and meeting Thomas for sure this time round; on the other, there was no way she could lose Guillaume, who was ... she cast about for the right word ... who was ... well, exactly like this armchair in which she was seated facing the analyst, with its straight back and its high, curved armrests that formed a structure around her, leaving her free to move while at the same time supporting her. Then she stood up, saying: "Of course, it's perfectly possible that I don't need this armchair at all and am about to discover that I can stand on my own two feet." But what if she couldn't? What if her body were to collapse with nothing to surround and support it any longer? For mysterious, unfathomable reasons, the analyst appeared to be urging her in the direction of Bordeaux.

Back in Sorge she patches things up with Guillaume because she knows that, sooner or later, she'll have to return to Bordeaux. She'll go there just on the off chance, just to gauge the situation and see what's really going on, to be sure the attraction Thomas holds for her isn't some outlandish fantasy conjured up by the streets of Sorge in summer. She can perfectly well imagine that, were she to see him somewhere else, under different conditions from those of the spell worked by the month of August, the whole edifice she had built up would collapse. It had happened to her before. As a teenager, she had fallen in love with a boy she had met while pony trekking in Ireland. The boy was a few years older than her, and she had daydreamed about him no end. Not as much as Thomas, not by a long way, for at the time she had far fewer images in her head. But still, she did find him very attractive. Being himself smitten, he had suddenly turned up that autumn in Paris, where Anna was living at the time, and the situation had been very awkward. She wasn't remotely attracted to him any more. She didn't know a thing about him and had no wish to know him. After his visit she had run off, standing him up at the rendezvous they'd fixed for the next day, unable at the time to explain herself, and too young and inexperienced to realize that such things happen and are not so very unusual.

Yes, Thomas was probably just a dream, and the extraordinary attraction she felt for him one of those castles in the air you're prone to building in the summer. When she was bare-legged in a short, light frock and her body was limber and tanned and she was strolling through the small town of Sorge with the countryside all around her, she felt closer to love than she did anywhere else on the planet. She liked the feel of the dry earth and the fine dust it left on your fingers, the warm pebbles, the rough stone walls she would run her hand over. She liked the bodily contact with things, she would happily have gone barefoot, and if she got scratched by brambles or stung by nettles while trying to reach in to gather a blackberry from a bush, she was glad of the little scratches and burns. She'd even wonder how you could live without them. Would she have fallen in love with Thomas had she met him in the cold? Would she have been so taken with him had she been wearing a scarf and wool gloves and drinking coffee in a closed room to the sound of a jukebox? Probably not, she thought to herself. They would have been separated by their thick winter coats, she would have been less pretty with her nose red from the cold, and less relaxed as a result, and she would have had no conception of her breasts or her forearms. She might never even have thought about his sex.

All summer they had made a game of what they were wearing. Each morning she would go out in a new dress, and since for a year or two now she had been continually renewing her wardrobe, she had some very pretty ones that summer, having suddenly become obsessed with dresses, as though dresses were what she had always wanted to wear, it had just taken her a long time to realize it. It had all begun with a white woolen one which made her into a very different type of woman from the one she usually came across as, and which she had worn until Christmas 2001. Then she had become fixated on having dresses for each season of the year, searching everywhere for them whenever she was staying in a big city, trying on any number, turning up a good many that were perfect for her, choosing them always flowing, soft, and strapless, in cheerful or subtle shades, and dancing about just above the knees. It was like a treasure hunt. Sometimes she would find two or three at once, it was an extravagance, she should have made do with just one, but all three suited her so well, she felt so happy in them, that she would slot them into her wardrobe, where they were so fine and so light that there was room for still others, should others turn up and prove similarly irresistible. She would slip one on, and the dress would shimmy down her body, hanging perfectly there, exactly her size, making her younger, droller, more unexpected.

That summer when she had sat drinking coffee with Thomas Lenz she had some real beauties: a red one with piping around the waist, a green and blue one that made her feel like a dancer, a very pale yellow one, and still others in which she would step out each morning feeling new and refreshed, as much to herself as to others. It was a frivolous pleasure but a deep one, designed not so much to please as to cheer her up. And because she was wearing one of these light summer frocks which had no straps or buttons and followed the curves of her body without ever constraining her at any point, she was girded for love. Thomas, on his side, was more understated, but she noticed at once the elegance with which he wore clothes that on anybody else would have seemed merely conventional and in good taste, but in his case were so well suited to his kind of presence as to be ideal. And so they conversed with their bodies and clothes that summer, pretending to turn a blind eye but secretly remarking an open-backed dress, a blue polo shirt, the pretty cut of a light-colored dress, the hang of a pair of old linen trousers. And each day they would renew their wardrobes, as if to surprise each other. But the change was so discreet—just a different dress with the same sandals, or a different sweatshirt with the same trousers—that it was like one of those conversations where you can always deny having said any such thing and pretend that the other person has misheard you.

AT THE END OF September, they decided to meet in Bordeaux to settle things once and for all. He was tired of his work being disrupted and of getting barely a wink of sleep for a month now; she was tired of being obsessed with him but having no way of verifying whether she was daydreaming or not. With much trepidation and bashfulness, a date was fixed. Right up to the last minute, he hoped she wouldn't come; right up to the last minute, she was afraid she would discover a man who bore only a passing resemblance to the Thomas she had loved so passionately, especially since he had left Sorge. Taking the train was a bit like visiting the dentist: she had to go through with it and see how it felt, the rest could be dealt with later. She lied to Guillaume for the first time in their life; she told him she was going to see a girlfriend. He believed her. (He half believed her.) It felt odd to be leaving, odd to have made that decision, but it had been settled long before, no? It dated from the previous summer. The story was twelve months gone: what on earth was taking place inside her? Why was she so gripped by an illusion? She imagined feeling let down, putting a brave face on it all and very gracefully drawing a line through this fanciful affair in such a way that neither of them need feel humiliated. She was capable of turning a situation around delicately, of so arranging things that neither of them would feel their pride had been hurt or their expectations dashed.

When she saw Thomas on the station platform in Bordeaux, he looked much smaller, and much less handsome, than she had remembered. He was nothing like the man she had seen in the streets of Sorge. For herself, she was too warmly dressed. But she put on a brave face, remarking inwardly on his size, he seemed a good four inches shorter than in Sorge where he had towered over her. She relaxed a little in the car, but was surprised to see him driving with a slight stoop and tried to recall whether he had driven like that on the road to the country inn last August; but no, at the time he hadn't been stooped, or not in her recollection at any rate. And yet here he was, hunched over the steering wheel, darting wary, somewhat fearful glances at her; she almost felt embarrassed. But despite feeling horribly let down, she was glad to be with him because it was where she was meant to be. And little by little he straightens up. They don't know one another, they know very little about each other, and yet she thinks to herself: he's my lover, it's the beginning of a story. She's feeling more relaxed, jokes good-humoredly with him, he's starting to relax, too.

She's booked a room in the hotel she likes; they'll meet later for dinner. In the warmth and comfort of her room she reviews the situation. No, she's no longer attracted to him; it was a mistake, then, but it doesn't matter. They'll dine together, it's no big deal, she'd been attracted to him in the past, so she'll spend a pleasant evening in his company, she'll ask him about his work and take an interest in it, men love that, then tomorrow they'll go for a stroll, and after that she'll take the train home and it'll all be over. At eight o'clock, while waiting for her in the street, he sends her an amusing text message that brings a smile to her lips. When she joins him he looks slightly taller than he had on the station platform. They dine outside on a restaurant terrace, spend a long time beating about the bush, then he asks her a strange question, point-blank, which she finds rather appealing. He's still not as tall or as elegant as he was in Sorge, but he's slowly gaining in stature. He walks her back to the hotel. There's no question of inviting him up, he no longer appeals to her at all on that front, he's just rather charming, rather mysterious, but nothing more than that. And in her room she phones Guillaume to tell him that everything is fine and that she's thinking of him, which is true.

The next day they've arranged to meet on a square and go for a walk outside Bordeaux. She makes her way there out of courtesy almost, but a little curious just the same, for he had seemed so flustered and apprehensive the night before. The square is huge, when she arrives there she looks around for him, sees him in the distance, and this time he resembles the man in Sorge. He's grown, he has that insulated air, he's wearing a pair of trousers which she notices from the opposite side of the square, trousers that have nothing very remarkable about them but remind her of the man she saw in Sorge. There's a place he wants to show her, but he takes the wrong road. In the car she does her best to be natural, vivacious even, but soon realizes that she has a very awkward, very alarming situation on her hands: it's as though she was with the wrong man. It's Guillaume she speaks to like this, Guillaume she uses these words and intonations with; nobody else. It's with Guillaume that she sits up front, bending forward to find a music station on the radio and commenting on the landscape. She steals a glance at Thomas. No, it's not Guillaume. She'd like to speak differently to him, address him differently, so as to distinguish him properly from Guillaume, but she can't. Something is compelling her to behave with Thomas exactly as she does with Guillaume, as if they had known each other for twenty years and shared a wealth of experience already. She tries repeatedly to redress the situation, her hand firmly on the tiller as when you're sailing on a rather choppy sea. But it's hard going, she pitches about a lot, on a knife edge all the time, with the risk that she will capsize at any moment and mistake him for Guillaume.

They drive around among big walled gardens with overhanging boughs and palm fronds. The sky is a harsh blue, she wishes to God she didn't feel quite so oppressed. He's silent and considerate, she needs to calm down and remind herself that she's gone for a drive with a new man she likes and finds attractive, that it's not a crime, that she's perfectly entitled to have a fling, even to cheat a little, everyone does it, there's nothing very shocking about it. Then she's tired of driving around, so they stop in the countryside to stretch their legs, as tongue-tied as ever, the pair of them, as if in thrall not to the question of whether to sleep together or not but to one they can't even formulate. They walk by a nondescript stream, and again he reminds her of someone. But who? Who did she walk by a stream with? Was it in a book? Was it in a novel that a man was walking by a stream and it made a powerful impression on her? Try as she might, she just can't retrieve it. It's there, on the tip of her tongue, when in the reeds, after going down into the stream, she rests her hand on his arm for a second in order to dry her feet with the other hand. He stands there without moving. This, too, reminds her of something. But what?

Who are you, then, Thomas Lenz, to have had this hold over Anna for so long now? Admittedly, she's a little crazy, as this story has shown—not to love you, for you possess any number of charms and graces, not least the ability to dance with her without trembling, but crazy to have found room in you for all her sacred images. Did you need to be vacant to allow her all that room? And compliant for her to carry on dreaming like this? Her folly hurtles back and forth like that terrifying fairground attraction she saw with Guillaume one day, in Bordeaux as it happens: suspended from a steel mast, a pod you could climb into and which could hold three or four people was suddenly propelled high into the air at the speed of a rifle shot, where it remained without moving for a few seconds before hurtling back to the earth at the same velocity. She wanted to go on it, but Guillaume refused. Who are you, then, Thomas Lenz, that the moment you appear she should catch fire like a torch, instantly fall into confusion and end up completely at a loss? Is this what always accompanies passion? This loss of one's former self? You're wary, you keep a close eye on her. You walk together in a field that in no time at all has ceased to be a field and is the garden of a parish priest, you don't know which direction to go in or where exactly you ought to be heading. Unlike Guillaume, you're not at all interested in landscapes; most of the time, you live deep inside yourself. You tell Anna about a friend at whose divorce proceedings you were summoned to testify: married to a charming young woman, the friend thought he would go mad with grief, since from the very first day she refused his advances and the marriage was never consummated. It's like a Barbey d'Aurevilly story, so Anna tells you about the haughty countess who, to avenge herself on her husband, who has been unfaithful, decides to prostitute herself in the most sordid manner possible, while making sure that word of it gets back to him. You talk about sex, in other words, without touching on the subject, and at no point, in fact, do you touch her. You know how to dance with her, but you also know how to fan her desire.

Who are you, then, Thomas Lenz? What a handsome face you have! What a handsome silhouette and aspect! Later, you'll hate it when she tells you she finds you handsome. It makes you feel awkward and uncomfortable. How do you manage to appear so measured in everything you do, to look as if you're alone all the time when you have a new woman at your side, descending with you into the courtyard of a wine merchant, where you've come to buy a few cases of a claret you like? It's as though you were insulated from the world by a halo, or by a suit of armor you always wear. Yes, you also resemble that famous painted knight in Sienna whom Anna had kept a postcard of for many years. And, talking of knights, you also resemble, of course, Goethe's knight riding through the forest. But that's quite enough. Please stop reminding me, pleads Anna, please stop reminding me continually of someone else. She would love to love Thomas Lenz, but she can't, because his form and image are continually taken up by someone else.

How relieved she is when there's something she doesn't like about him! She's not wild about his hands, for example, they're disappointing—slender, but not long enough in her book. To give herself a rest, she observes his hands on the steering wheel. And she ends up liking these hands that she finds so restful. Would she like him to descend on her all of a sudden? In one fell swoop? Probably. Otherwise, there's this towering void between them. But the idea never seems to cross his mind. He does things one at a time, like in those courtships of old where, after a lengthy engagement during which you kiss just one time perhaps, right at the very end, you move on to more serious matters only once you are married. That's the time frame he inhabits. The traditional one. Were she suddenly to strip naked before him, he'd be astonished, but he wouldn't move a finger in response. Thomas Lenz, dear knight, she thinks to herself, what an odd fellow you are. You probably believe in mystic marriages and unbridled love, you may not have that many desires, I dare say you're horribly sentimental. She's completely at sea, but he's not, since he accompanies her to the station at the appointed hour for her train back to Sorge. He's the kind of man you have to marry, she thinks to herself, an idea she finds droll, having never wished to marry. He wants all of her, all to himself, forever, he won't budge on that. Thomas Lenz, what a curious fellow you are.

In the train she falls asleep, she's exhausted. Thomas Lenz exhausts her. She's going to put a stop to it. In any case, he's going away for three weeks for his research, and they've agreed that during those three weeks they won't communicate. It's better that way, she thinks. Yes, it's better that way. But the very next day, she misses him already and sends him an email before he leaves; he replies at once, as if hiding behind the screen, waiting for her. They're simmering, positively bubbling over with passion, so why doesn't she follow him? Why doesn't she drop everything and run off with him? She has no idea. She's capable of doing something like that. But she doesn't do it. Why? She lets him go, lets him leave for three weeks, it feels like an eternity, but then she was the one who had suggested a pause, time in which to think things over. Before leaving her on the platform at Bordeaux he'd given her a few CDs of music he enjoys. She listens to them a lot, wallowing in it as if he was there, contained in the music, and all the more intoxicated by it as she's been drinking a bit too much; way too much, in fact. She always drinks too much when she's in love like this. It had begun ten years earlier with that man she'd been infatuated with who had always eluded her; she had started drinking, rather too much at times, in order to feel connected to him. With no alcohol inside her they were cruelly apart; with alcohol inside her, pitching her thoughts about, opening the doors to her heart, allowing her emotions to wash back and forth and easing the tension in her shoulders, she felt as if she was touching his body, joined with him at last. It might even have been better in a way than actually being together. And so, for the entire duration of their yearlong affair, she had often been joined with this man whom she had never touched, apart from one time, just one time, when she had stroked his head at a moment when, for all his desire, he hadn't a clue what to do to reach her.

With Thomas, however, it's different. Thomas would love to be touched, only in his case, it seems, there can be no turning back afterward. The man really does need to loosen up. Or is it Anna for once who needs to loosen up? Isn't she the one with this idea in her head that, should she touch him, there can be no turning back? She had never felt that way with Guillaume. She could touch Guillaume and be touched by him, and though they advanced in their life together without dwelling on the past, she wasn't cut off from that past, it could move freely inside her, rear up all of a sudden, infuse her thoughts and deeds, wash back and forth as it pleased. With Thomas it was as if she had to leave all of her past life behind and step into a different world. Is that what marriage is, she wonders? Yes, probably. You leave behind the world of your childhood, your parents, your playthings, your pastimes, you go through a secret ceremony where you put on a particular dress that you'll never wear again in your life, and once the ceremony is over, you step into a different world. That was probably why she had never wanted to marry: she lives with her past and her childhood toys.

Thomas holds out for three weeks: no text, no letter, no phone call. For Anna, it's more difficult. Down there, she imagines, in the heat of northern Australia where he's doing his research, he has forgotten her. It's so easy to forget when you're traveling; half the time when you're abroad, you wonder how you could ever have had such thoughts back home. She'd noticed, in fact, that you had only to spend a bit of time with friends whose lifestyle was slightly different from yours—less dreamy and more practical—for the enormous daydream you had been toiling at in the secrecy of your solitude suddenly to be exposed for what it was. How often she had felt this when visiting her friends the elderly couple. Their apartment was so spacious, so peaceful and awash with light, that the moment she stepped through the door it seemed hard to believe she'd had so much on her mind these last few days at home; here, it seemed so easy just to live. She glanced round at the bright curtains, the beautifully kempt rugs, the elegant furniture; her elderly friends didn't smoke, of course, and they didn't drink like she did, there were very few books, lots of photos of children and grandchildren, flowers, and the circulation of air and light in the enormous, gaily colored room made it feel almost like a garden. Perhaps that's what Eden was. Had an archangel with wings and a white toga appeared at the door to the salon to announce lunch she wouldn't have been terribly surprised. Why couldn't she live like this herself? The house she shared with Guillaume was by no means lacking in gaiety and color and beautiful objects, but there were so many books, just the two of them, and that little split which had started in August 2002 and which they both tried not to attach too much importance to.

What does Anna do with her time, then, while Thomas is away? As always she daydreams, and rather more than usual. She neglects her articles and exhibitions and drifts about the house straightening pictures and sorting through cupboards. Guillaume tries to shake her up: she should get back to work, why doesn't she go down to Bordeaux where her friends always seem to do her good and stimulate her? She looks at him in astonishment. Is he trying to tell her he has understood something? No, of course he isn't, it's not his style. Guillaume is plainspoken. He has so much faith in her it would never occur to him that her daydreams now make up ninety percent of her thoughts. The music Thomas likes, which she puts on the moment Guillaume goes out, brings her closer to Thomas and Australia, and makes her feel so in love with him that it's as if her whole body were rustling. Then Guillaume comes home, she hasn't touched a drop of alcohol for two hours and has rinsed her mouth out and taken a cold shower; she's so happy with Guillaume, and so in love with him, too, that if only he would stay home all the time she wouldn't dream about Thomas. She thinks of asking him to stay home all the time. His handsome body which has always reminded her of freshly baked bread would stand in the way. If Guillaume's body was standing there day and night between her and Thomas, she'd forget all about Thomas. But she doesn't dare ask this of Guillaume. Perhaps she's not so keen to be separated from what she imagines to be Thomas's body after all.

The days go by, she can no longer recall the precise date on which he left, nor the precise date on which he is due back, nor if he had really informed her of the date. It feels like a long time has passed. At least a month, surely? So she sends him a cautious text message, just to see if he's there and still loves her. He replies with a rambling, half-hearted email, to which she replies with an email that's even more rambling and half-hearted, whereupon, as luck would have it, he flips over like a carp, furious all of a sudden: if she's that half-hearted, she can go to hell, to which she replies that she's not half-hearted at all and tells him how miserable she's been these last few days, whereupon he tells her how fortunate he is to love her, and away they go again. You're an odd fish, Thomas Lenz. Why, in that case, did you keep her waiting all this time? Because she asked you to remain silent? Yes, it's an excellent reason, but do you always do as women ask? Do you really have no desires or free will of your own? No? You'd rather be a victim? You're so mindful of a woman's freedom that you refuse to interfere in any way? Your enormous respect for a woman's desires does you credit, but isn't one of a lover's functions to force things a little from time to time? And even to do the truly courteous thing and take responsibility for an act, rather than leave it up to your partner? You're a peculiar fellow, Thomas Lenz, wanting to bear no responsibility in love.

Is Anna troubled by this? Not in the least. She's far too in love with Thomas to be able to think straight. She's bowled over by his chasteness and reserve, to say nothing of that impassioned outcry—in Australia he'd been sick with longing, he had told her—which she knows to be genuine, not in the least put-on, but which, were she more dispassionate, would give her food for thought regarding Thomas Lenz's personality. She finds it heartrending and would like to protect that child, bring him joy, permit him to be more active in love. She would like to set him free. She remembers how Guillaume had laid siege to her, his determination had been a delight to behold. She had given him to understand, of course, that she was attracted to him, and then waited for him the way deer in the forest in the rutting season come sniffing the air for a moment before disappearing back into the woods as if their mind was on other things. It was the stag's job to come and find them, the stag's job to flush them out. They will pretend for a moment to find these approaches tiresome, staring at each other with an astonished and ever so slightly indignant air, but the stag pays no heed, he's seen it all before, and two hours later they'll be gathered round him, pining, lovestruck, desiring only that he mount them, because that is nature's great religion. Guillaume was perfect in the role of stag: combative, headstrong, paying no heed to displays of coyness or even to farewell letters, which he considered so much hot air. He wanted this woman, and, without resorting to any kind of subterfuge, he had her because he wanted her.

Anna, however, is in love. Thomas has such a handsome face. She can see her reflection there, as if in a mirror. She can see why he's so scared, and why he's unable to take responsibility for anything: it's the story of his childhood secret, which he has yet to mention but which she has sensed, and on and around which their love is built. She knows this; and he, no doubt, knows that she knows, since it was the child in him she would address whenever they were chatting over coffee in Sorge. That's why he puts himself in her hands. How can you walk away from a man who puts himself in your hands? Who looks to you for the coming of spring? Who looks to you to release him from the woe that was his life? Who only half believes in his life, if that, but nevertheless, since meeting you, believes in it a wee bit more just the same? How can you leave him stranded there when you know the good it will do him to be cosseted and loved, and the good it will do you to dispense a little happiness? They meet on a plane where there are no words. They've exchanged hundreds of emails, they both write beautifully—believe me, their exchanges are so interesting they'd be worth publishing. But where they meet there are no words. And it's precisely this lack of the very possibility of words that binds them together body and soul and makes them crazy about each other.

THEY DECIDE TO SLEEP together to find out what's really going on. There's something clinical—something comical almost—about the whole business, and it's Anna, of course, who takes charge of the proceedings. They're in love, they're crazy about each other, they need to sleep together to ascertain the facts, they can see about the rest later: either they'll realize they are incompatible, which is more than likely, or they'll be happy, in which case they can sort the rest out later. Needless to say, arranging the rendezvous proves very complicated. She hunts around for hotels in Paris, visits a good ten rooms, sees some nice ones and books a few, but it's strange to be choosing a pretty room in a hotel for a rendezvous with someone you're in love with—it's vulgar, it's embarrassing, no, she really can't go through with it. So he starts looking for hotel rooms instead, places with a bit of charm, but it's hard because he doesn't know her tastes all that well and finds the whole idea of looking for a hotel room repugnant, so he stops. She starts all over again. Instead of Paris, how about Marseilles or Lille or Brest? She scouts around in Marseilles and Lille and Brest, towns she has never visited with Guillaume. All the same, it would be odd to meet in Brest or Lille solely for the purpose of sleeping together; why not meet in Bordeaux, it would be so much simpler? Yes, indeed, why not Bordeaux after all? he agrees. At the same time, Bordeaux *is* the town he lives in; sharing his apartment with him, there is also his son: how about somewhere close to Bordeaux? If it's close to Bordeaux, it's bound to be nice. It would be close to Bordeaux, and at the same time it wouldn't be Bordeaux. He finds something. In this instance, then, he has shouldered the responsibility and influenced the course of events slightly. He must really want me, she thinks to herself.

A date is fixed for the room, with sex pencilled in. They both find the decision a bit forced and artificial, but what else can they do, they have very little choice in the matter. In the meantime, he'll come and pick her up at the station in Bordeaux. What state of mind is she in during the journey? Curious, no doubt. Extremely curious. Because ever since that second coffee in Sorge it's what she has wanted: to be naked at his side. She takes the train to Bordeaux—for Guillaume, she has gone to see a girlfriend—Thomas is waiting for her, near Bordeaux he takes her to the place where they have decided to see each other naked and touch each other at last. Naturally, he has chosen a rather peculiar spot built round with walls, but that's the way it is. It's quite something, this moment just before you sleep with someone you have been fantasizing about for more than a year, with whom you have already been through so much, talked so much, exchanged so many emails and text messages, and with whom you have discussed everything under the sun except, as you are both perfectly aware, the one thing that brings you together. He's scared, of course, so to reassure him she acts detached, but she's scared, too, and when, many thousands of hours later, they at last find themselves in the room together, no reader who has been paying attention will imagine that it's to jump on each other. No, they don't jump on each other. She still has her dress on, he hasn't removed his jacket yet, he places a hand on her shoulder, and she screams, she howls, she cries, she trembles. No, don't cry, don't tremble like that, he says. But she howls as if she had been touched by a flame, by something unbearable, she screams and she cries. He sits on the bed and tells her stories, she listens, she asks questions like a little child who is being told a bedtime story before going to sleep. He replies the way you reply to a little child. He carries on with his stories, she carries on with her questions, and her voice is that of a twelve-year-old, then an eight-year-old, then six. He replies as if she were a little child. They sleep naked together, but she's not afraid and neither is he, he tells her stories, she asks him questions, her voice is that of a twelve-year-old, then an eight-year-old, then six, he replies and explains things in the stories to her, she gives him a little kiss before falling asleep. That's how they come together. There are times when people's love lives just don't make sense.

The following morning they have breakfast together on the patio. She hadn't noticed the previous evening that the place was a guesthouse. Thomas is standing next to her, and while sipping her coffee she squeezes his leg. It's like the leg of a gladiator, she thinks, and she tells Thomas this, who laughs. She thinks continually of Guillaume, because he's the only person in twenty years she has ever found herself having breakfast with after spending the night together. But Thomas is sufficiently quiet, sufficiently discreet and retiring, for her not to feel too unhappy thinking about Guillaume. What's marvelous about Thomas is that he doesn't behave like a man in love. He's gentle and attentive, of course, but at no point does he kiss her or fling his arms around her. It's as if they hadn't slept together. He remains withdrawn, insulated from the world, in his formidable trousers, it's as though she hadn't screamed and cried that much when he had ever so lightly grazed her shoulder. They can relax at last. They've told each other everything.

Once, in the days when her sister was unwell (the one who would later kill herself), Anna had been with her one night at the emergency psychiatric unit of a hospital. Among the patients was a very beautiful young woman who was utterly distraught and would clutch at the coats of doctors walking past, screaming at them with unparalleled force, "I love you!" "I love you!" Her face was at once radiant and tormented, inspired. Were the doctor to pull away without responding, the young woman's passionate cries of love would persist until he had disappeared around the end of the corridor. She then seemed to calm down. Were another doctor to appear suddenly from an office, her declarations of love would leap forth once more, with the same truthfulness, the same urgency and force.

In the afternoon, they walk together along a path bordered with yellow reeds where, from time to time, herons drift softly by. It pains her, it pains her greatly, to be walking there with him, and not with

Guillaume; and that pain will be inscribed in her for months to come. Nearly every time she's with him, albeit of her own free will, of her own desire, it will pain her, pain her continually, to see him standing in Guillaume's shoes, to herself be putting him in those shoes: in her brain it's a sort of nightmare every time. And yet she has to go through with it, she knows she has to pass through that dark night. It's dangerous, though, far more dangerous for her than for these two men, who will also suffer, of course, but she—she is risking death, or something worse than death.

He's alarmed by the expression on her face and is trying to understand. "You look tormented," he tells her. No one has ever told her her face could look tormented. "Don't be silly," she says. "I promise you," he says. He's like a fond, tenderhearted father with a child who's just had a horrible nightmare. He loves her, he has truly fallen in love with her, but because he doesn't know why she sometimes has that look on her face, everything he does or says scares him. He wouldn't want a word or a deed of his to trigger that look. So with each timorous movement of his hand—for a long time he will barely touch her—he asks: does this hurt? And how about this: does this hurt? "Don't be silly," she says with a shrug, laughing as if he was the dim-witted one. But he persists, he knows something very odd is causing her all this pain, he's confronted with it daily and would like to make sense of it, would like to be able to pin it down.

And so this passion, which had begun like a storybook romance—the moment they set eyes on each other they fall madly in love—enters upon a dark night and a turmoil of a rather different order. He doesn't call it quits, though. Is it simply out of obstinacy, now that he has met a woman he loves? Or is it because he, too, must pass through a dark night of sorts? She turns him inside out like a glove. "You make me think differently," he tells her, "you've changed a lot about me, everything I believed in and built my life around is upended or under threat." Guillaume had said this, too. Her love for Guillaume, however, was all of a piece, she was with him wholeheartedly, so he could go about his transformation at his own good speed. Whereas this poor Thomas, she throws herself at him and then backs away, makes outlandish declarations and then wriggles free, pines for his body like the promised land and then starts trembling. He'll have to be quite something, Thomas, to stay the course.

She had always known that one day she would have to pass through a dark night of the soul. She had known it since reading the mystics in her youth, and later from novels she'd read. And some of her friends knew this, too, the dearest among them being

Pierre, whom she had met when she was twenty and who had remained very close to her ever since. Pierre had always dreaded the idea of something happening to Anna. He saw her leading a happy life, thought well of Guillaume, and took an interest in her work; there was little for him to be alarmed by, and most of the time he wasn't. But the moment Anna departed slightly from her usual conduct—buying too many dresses, say, or wanting a dog, or suddenly developing a nasty pain in her shoulder, or taking an interest in an artist's work for no good reason he could see—something in him would spring to attention. For Guillaume, these quirks were signs of Anna's open-mindedness, of her independence and curiosity, and he would praise her vitality. Pierre, on the other hand, disapproved when she changed her ways, for in Anna's case, he thought, it was a bad sign. Without really acknowledging it, and without their ever discussing the matter, Pierre was afraid she would do something insane one day. What exactly, he would have been hard put to say, but he'd always feared that moment when she would no longer be the Anna he knew but someone else, as if the one was contained in the other.

And here she was—she, who had always been contained—looming up out of nowhere. Here she was, rearing her head in her somewhat outlandish emails to Thomas, her behavior toward Thomas, her feelings and emotions for Thomas, when for everybody else, for Guillaume and Pierre and the world at large, she was the same woman she'd always been. Thomas, in short, knew a woman whom no one had seen before, or had just caught a fleeting glimpse of perhaps. He was dealing with a woman who no longer knew a thing about herself, who had ceased to have a past, as it were, or any experience on which she might draw. She was like a great gale blowing suddenly in every direction, bending the branches one way, then opening them out again and bending them in the opposite direction; she would wear the dresses she had bought over the past year as if they were flaming torches and she herself a figure on a playing card available in ten different outfits. And while the pain she would feel went about its work—a pain she could at the same time appraise, measuring its advance—each day she would choose from one hour to the next whether to consent to it or not; and for the time being she consented to it because she knew that its function, if all went well, was to transform her into the dawn.

You can be spared unbridled love and its torments: you just have to say no. No to the mess and chaos, no to the loss of self, no to the transformation. In that case you remain within the confines of a more bearable life, and much of the time she was tempted by this. To return wholeheartedly to Guillaume like the soul returning to paradise, to extend their home and go walking on the mule tracks once again, to continue to put together good articles, and perhaps even a book—why not?—on the exhibitions and art she loved, to spend more time with people with somewhat traditional, conventional life styles, people who invariably did her a world of good, to buy trousers for a change instead of dresses. Yes, within those bounds she would grow and put down roots and dispense a little happiness around her, and in no time at all Thomas would be nothing but a daydream dwindling away into the past, like a distant silhouette on a road which, when you glance back a hundred yards further on to see if it can still be glimpsed, is barely visible. She could do that, it wasn't even all that difficult; but then something quite terrifying and unexpected occurred: Guillaume left her. And for this to happen in the middle of the book, it could only have occurred at the very center of her being.

ADMITTEDLY, SHE HAD A dream. And for months, for more than a year now, she had been nursing that dream in secret. So great had it grown that it henceforth filled the entire cage, with its wings poking out, so that she couldn't really hide it from Guillaume any longer. So one winter's afternoon when they were at a bit of a loose end, they decided to drive out to the forest. The snow was dazzling, with glints of blue, and lay thick on the paths. Guillaume eased the car into the woods and pulled over; they would make their way through a small stretch of forest and he would show her a valley she had almost certainly never seen before. They were buttoned up tight, the two of them. Where they would usually have talked freely of this and that, Anna's hand wrapped in the great warm hand of Guillaume, this time they had difficulty speaking, a situation so unheard-of that they both felt very scared. They tried to slip back into their usual banter the way you try to place your feet in your own footprints, but they knew each other too well for either of them to be taken in. Horrified, Anna could feel the fabric of their life tearing apart; what held them together now was little more than rags. Guillaume's voice changed as he asked her to explain what was going on; he asked her this without violence, gently even, but his voice had changed completely, it wasn't the voice he usually spoke to her in, it was like an official voice. What could she say? Where should she begin? There was no place to begin. She couldn't say, like a character in a sitcom: "I love someone else," since she still loved him, Guillaume. Perhaps she might have said: "I also love someone else." But "love" wasn't the right word for it. No, it was something else, but what? "I've fallen in love" was no good either, it sounded like something out of a soap opera. "The apparition of a man has cast a spell on me, and I am living under that spell:" those would have been suitable words. But Guillaume's face had hardened, his voice was that of a manager, a boss, a high-court judge, the tenderness it had always held was gone; Anna was chilled to the core by the transformation, which she would never have thought possible.

She said nothing, not so much because she was fearful, but because she didn't have the words to describe what had been taking place inside her for months now. Had she known what was taking place inside her, she would have told him, no doubt; and, understanding Anna, he would have understood. But it was the first time he had seen her without words to define something, and for that reason, being wholly bound up in his emotions, instead of telling himself that she was momentarily at a loss for words no doubt, as he would have done had he been feeling less anxious, he thought she was deliberately avoiding the issue. For the first time, he thought like an ordinary man and ascribed ordinary behavior to her—he, who had always known exactly what it was she was and wasn't saying, and was wedded to her the way a vase is wedded to the water it encloses. They wound their way laboriously through the wood, they were no longer holding hands, and when he paused for a moment to gaze up at the top of a tree and she came over to give him a little kiss on the cheek, he turned away and resembled an eagle all of a sudden. Never before had this happened, not once in twenty years had he turned away when she had come up to him. Their clothes, the damp tree trunks, and the stones were black; the rest of the landscape was a dazzling white. When they pulled out onto the road, which they both knew like the back of their hand, he went the wrong way and they drove for miles in the wrong direction without either of them noticing. In the car, he had recovered a bit of his warmth, but it was obvious something terrible had happened. For the first time, they had been truly separated, far more so than in the episode with the seaside apartment, which, compared to the great rift in the black and white forest, was altogether insignificant. They had been separated, and for Anna it was not just shocking, it was unthinkable, quite simply inconceivable.

He went away for a few days; she cast around for the right words. Not that she wanted to smooth things over, to spare him at any cost, nor to sugarcoat her own feelings; no, she wanted to do what she had always done and tell him the truth. But whenever she reflected on what was going on with Thomas, she found it impossible—she, who usually had no difficulty expressing herself—to find words for the situation. It was as if none of the things that are typically said about love—about the feelings and emotions you experience—were suitable. And so she dug herself into a hole. She withdrew into a silence that wasn't like her, and from this he deduced that she had a guilty secret, which in a sense she did; but he also concluded, rather too hastily, that she no longer loved him, since she loved someone else. Only to women, it seems, are these distinctions in love immediately comprehensible. When Anna confided in her women friends in Paris (in Sorge she hadn't breathed a word to anyone), all of them said: yes, of course, nothing could be simpler, you love Guillaume and you're in love with Thomas. It seemed so clear to her women friends that you could love one man and at the same time long for another. They also told her that one day she would have to choose, but that she needn't worry about it for the moment, time would decide. But again Anna felt this wasn't quite right. It wasn't a question of choosing but of jumping clear of tragedy, that inextricable knot in which all our limbs are tangled.

And who else but Guillaume could help her to do this? He'd always been there for her, had never left her to fend for herself in a difficult situation. She would tell him about the attraction she felt, she would tell him about Jude the Obscure and all these figures, the image that was continually eluding her: he would understand perfectly. It was only his eagle head in the snow that scared her slightly. But it was possible that she had been dreaming or that he had only had that head because she had said nothing. Besides, Guillaume necessarily knows the whole story from the beginning, since he knows everything about her and loves her perfectly. The moment he comes home, then, she tells him the story: Jude the Obscure, the images, the attraction she feels, she runs through the various details. Suddenly, Guillaume is no longer Guillaume, he's someone else. She's appalled, petrified: he has obviously misunderstood her, if she runs through it all again he'll realize there's been a misunderstanding. So she tells the story again, in the same way that people will sometimes mutilate a body or tear out a heart without understanding why it's convulsing and bleeding. Guillaume has stood up, he's packing his bags, he's leaving, he says, it's all over. And it doesn't even occur to Anna to run after him or to try to hold him back: a separation is impossible since each is contained in the other.

In their bedroom she finds herself very hesitantly touching things—the lampshade, the bedspread, the rim of the washbasin—as if to make sure that all these objects are real, do indeed have bodies, that she hasn't simply dreamed them up. He has misunderstood her, but it's of no great importance, he'll go and sleep at his parents' house, sulk perhaps for a few days—well, it's a bit more than just sulking, his pride has been hurt, what do you expect, he's a grown man—but tomorrow or the next day he'll send her a text or he'll phone, or she will, and they'll meet up and everything will be back as it was. Feeling reassured, she rings Thomas and they talk about their love for each other, which has nothing whatever to do with the love she and Guillaume feel. Nevertheless, she falls asleep with a slight veil over her eyes, a slight feeling of unease. Guillaume can't seriously have walked out on her, surely? He can't abandon her, can he? The idea's almost laughable—Guillaume, abandon her? Come now! But she sees his eagle head in the snow. Has she really just committed the greatest folly of her life?

The days go by. She rings, he picks up, he always used to pick up at once when she rang, even when he was busy in a meeting on the other side of the globe. She always came first. He's unhappy, he's suffering, but he picks up. She tries to make him understand that there's no reason to be unhappy, that there's been a mistake. Yes, she has this relationship with Thomas, but so what? Does it prevent her from loving him, too? From loving him first and foremost? It's not that she doesn't really love Thomas, she loves him differently, quite differently, it's absurd to compare, Thomas isn't a rival, he's like another country, how can you demand of someone that they love only one country when they're fond of two? Isn't it perfectly normal—healthy even—to be capable of loving two countries? Guillaume still doesn't understand her. Perhaps it's a question of words? Of the different meanings they attach to certain words? But she'd always thought they spoke the same language. It's beginning to dawn on her now: when he says "love," he means being in love, being overcome with desire and excitement. That's not what she means. When she says "love," she means encompassing the other or being inside them, knowing them inside out almost and feeling perfectly happy with them. So, no, she can't be said to love Thomas in that case; she's strongly attracted to him, it's a fact, but loving, that comes later, it's when you have reached the stage where you're living one inside the other, and she certainly hasn't reached that point with Thomas. But why doesn't Guillaume understand this? It's so simple. Before, she had never needed to explain anything to him, whatever they were talking about, they understood each other perfectly; in twenty years they'd never had a single misunderstanding, and they must have had a serious spat only twice: one time because he held political views she didn't share; the other time she can't even remember why. Their first quarrel had been in Naples, it was about ten years ago, he had stormed out of their hotel room to go and walk around outside: she had provoked him by swallowing a large glass of whisky straight down in front of him, but the sight of him storming out had proved too much for her and she had gone after him in a fit of anger, clutching his hand, full of anger and love, as he was too. The second time was in the Dordogne where someone had lent them a rather dreary cottage. Again, he had stormed out to go walking on his own in the pouring rain. But apart from those two times in twenty years, no, they had never misunderstood each other, had never been unhappy together: whatever one of them might do or feel, the other one would understand.

The others seem to find it credible that Guillaume should abandon her. They're surprised, moreover, by her use of the word "abandon." Why not the word "leave," they ask? But then they don't quite grasp the nature of Guillaume and Anna's love. Nor for that matter does Thomas, who in situations like this thinks you must decide and says he is willing to bow out if that's what Anna prefers, for he wants her to be happy and understands Guillaume's reaction, he would have felt the same. In short, it's as if the whole world was incapable of understanding the distinctiveness of Guillaume and Anna's love. It's not the kind of romance you find in a film or a novel, between a man and a woman who love one another, are unfaithful, suffer, and part. It's a loftier form of love than that, high up on a mountain ridge, as it were, and not contingent on anything, and certainly not on desire, for example. It's above such things. True, they had made love a lot—and with what ardor, what joy and understanding! And true, too, this had played a major role in their affection for each other. But what really counted was hiking in the mountains together or going to see a giant anthill one day and standing there hand in hand among the rolling meadows. With no one else in the world would she have ventured along those dirt tracks; with no one else in the world would it have given her so much joy. Once, after tramping about all day in the boxwood, the heat, the scree, the sweet-smelling plants, the storm turning overhead, the only solution on a path blocked by impenetrable brushwood was to hand their way down the steep, stony mountainside, their bellies pressed against rocks that would come loose and go crashing to the bottom of the ravine, echoing for miles around. She wasn't scared; she was laughing. Nothing could go wrong since Guillaume was there. And sure enough, whether making their way across a snowfield below a glacier, or some spot where the path gave out but where they were forced to pass, with only the abyss below, among plants so soft or short you couldn't get a hold on any of them, nothing unfortunate would ever befall them because they were together, because it was them, because it was Guillaume and Anna.

Abandon her? You can't simply abandon someone who is everything to you, as you are to her. At a pinch you can ignore her, withdraw for a time into your anger and dignity and leave her to her little extravaganza. But to become so detached that you risk no longer loving her one day? Come now! It's impossible. What will become of the mountains without them? Will the landscape still exist if they no longer scale it in every direction? All those forest paths with their all but invisible wild animals, the millions of little stones, all the tree trunks they would clasp, the sun that would make them sweat, the icy water that would turn their bare feet into cold blocks of stone, all the whistles and sticks he would carve for her, the little cushions he would make for her among the springy, coarse-textured plants on the slopes. No, it exists for all eternity.

AT THE SAME TIME, there's Thomas. And regardless of whether Guillaume is present or not, regardless of whether Guillaume returns for a moment to their home in Sorge, where—it's most peculiar—he almost has the air of an outsider, a figure from the past, Thomas, for all that he remains silent, seems slightly more flesh and blood. Oh, he's still nine parts fiction, Anna barely knows him, and when she does touch him, it's still only Guillaume she's touching through him. But when he tells her about the best friend of his youth, Luc, who at thirty killed himself, and about their joyful and infinitely precious friendship, he laughs like a child, though not much given to laughter in other circumstances. Is it because of Luc, or because of that laughter perhaps: for the first time, she no longer sees Thomas as an image. And what did

Luc say? What did Luc do? she asks. He tells the story again, adding details, turning back to that fullness of joy as if it were a perpetual summer in a white house with the windows open to the sun and the warm air, and Luc running wild and Thomas following behind, released. When he talks about Luc, it's Thomas she has standing before her, not Guillaume. She feels herself loving this friend together with him, this friend who did him so much good. Luc's death had cast a pall over Thomas. Never again had he felt so much joy.

The inroads Thomas is making are so discreet you would think he was whispering. He barely brushes against her, barely risks an advance: he's well schooled in the art of tragedy. Her own eyes in the meantime have multiplied tenfold, like the eyes on a peacock's tail. One gesture too many, a single word out of place, and she'll send him flying over the parapet of that terrifying dam he had taken her to see near Bordeaux, which they had traversed on foot without batting an eyelid. The spectacle? A huge bulwark of stone, all of a piece, in one great block, a bulwark to put the fear of God into you; and far below, right at the very bottom, a still, small, turquoise lake. They walk along the top of the dam, Thomas pats a dog they meet, he doesn't say a word about the wall, not a word about the lake, he barely sets eyes on them in fact, he's silent and he's present. He's waiting.

During all the weeks that follow, moreover, should he be so unfortunate as to take a great step forward and risk an advance, she immediately jumps back. "You'd think we were playing chess," she says. "Oh really?" he asks. His gestures are the conventional ones of the old-fashioned lover: little gifts, albeit ever so discreet, little kindnesses, little pamperings so impalpable that it was like being grazed by a feather. "Thomas Lenz," she tells him, "you're quite some ladies' man, I must say." He's nothing of the sort, of course. He's not expert in the sense of mindful, calculating, organized; he's expert because he loves her and because he wants her. He's not to make a sound, not to stir other than in a dreamlike manner? Very well, he won't make a sound, and if he does stir slightly it will be in a dream and nowhere else. Consequently, Anna relaxes a little, relaxes a lot, in fact, and lo! he messes up, piles on the errors, all of a sudden he's gone much too far with his words and gestures, she slams all the doors to the apartment, storms out, shuts herself away in Sorge, wants to get back together with Guillaume — Guillaume who, unlike Thomas, understands her and knows exactly how to love her. Thomas holds out. He waits. She returns with a thousand conditions; he accepts the thousand conditions and even adds one she had overlooked. Thomas Lenz, you're a lot stronger than it might appear.

There are times when she almost misses Jude the Obscure, who had so captured her imagination. Just for the thrill of it, just to remain in that part of her mind where she risks nothing, where everything is in the form of images still, she plays back the film of Thomas appearing on the streets of Sorge. At home, there's Guillaume standing guard and striking the hours—present and dependable; in the streets there's Anna and her summer dresses, the market square in the noonday sun, and, in the distance, coming down from the horizon like some mysterious, avenging cowboy riding into a town where everything is boarded up, deserted, silent, the slim, tall, empty silhouette of Thomas. Sometimes it's better that way—better not to go up to him, not to address him, to let him make his way into town like this, to observe from a distance this presence that will change everything. And while she's chatting in her dream with friends and acquaintances she has run into among the market stalls, her heart and mind are entirely taken up with the advance of this silhouette, and with the order and disorder which nobody—it's incredible—seems to realize it will bring in its wake.

"Look!" she wants to say when she bumps into Jean or Sylvie or Anne-Marie. "Look! Can't you see that the whole town has changed? That the lines have shifted?" But everyone seems to think it's a perfectly ordinary market day; the usual conversations are being held with more or less the same words, more or less the same exclamations and intonations. Goodness! she almost regrets that Jude the Obscure has arrived in town; it was so nice before, so homely and down to earth, the streets were huge if a little empty, the priest would stroll by on his way to the service, the tobacconist would smile, each year families would add a child or two to their number, the children would grow, little alterations would be made to the town, a gym would be built or a house torn down, another home would be converted into a shop, nothing changed much, you only had to endure and it was all very pleasant. What would have become of her had Jude not turned up? She would have gone on with her quiet, happy life. Had she reached the end of something with Guillaume, therefore? Was twenty years their measure? The measure of their love? Had they gone too far in their knowledge of one another? Their openness? Their suitability? Jude the Obscure is like a knife cutting through all that. Someone ought to warn you that your life can be turned upside down, transformed beyond recognition, by a dream. You wouldn't be quite so taken aback, you would have weapons to defend yourself, time to prepare.

And so she sinks into a powerful melancholy. Anna Lore, surely you're not going to take your own life merely because of a love story? Because of two love stories that refuse to meet? I don't know, says Anna. I'd prefer not to, of course, but what is to be done when, like Ravaillac in his torment, I'm pulled in opposite directions, the tension being exactly equal on either side? What is to be done? It's such a strain. On one side, you have the mountains and their fragrances, which I certainly can't live without; on the other, Jude the Obscure and his black doublet on the high streets of Bordeaux. The two sides are incompatible, I can't combine them as I'd have so loved to do; I thought I might be able to alternate them: one day darkness, one day light, one day reverie, the next day something different, one day the freshly baked bread of Guillaume's body, the next this hard slim flesh that makes me tremble. But it's clearly not possible, so what does that leave? To stay locked up in my room like a nun? Why not? That might be a solution, but how shall I live without love when I'm so fond of loving? I need those highways along which so much flows—words, riveting conversations, that communion with others without which I cease to exist. Oh, I can strive to be alone if I must, to live without a man is no big deal, it can even be quite restful, but to live without the wondrous intensity of love, that dialogue so rich that it fills your life—how could I? I'm not interested in solitude.

Anna Lore, think for a second. Your mother took her own life, your sister took her own life, at exactly your age: are you really so eager to follow in the family footsteps? No, of course not, says Anna Lore, with a shrug and a faint smile. Beware of the dead, they can drag you down at times, they're not always a force for good in life. You think you have buried them deep beneath the earth, you lay flowers on their graves, you're glad to be alive, then all of a sudden you turn a corner one day in August and find them standing there, calling for you, holding out their arms to you; and since of course you were very fond of your mother, and very fond of your sister, you're tempted to join them in these womanly comings and goings, which have other virtues than the comings and goings of men. Watch your step, Anna Lore, think carefully now, try to understand what it is you are doing by dreaming too much, dreaming far too much. At which point Anna thinks of her buried sister, and of her mother, no doubt long since turned to dust. They are laid together in the same crypt, which has made them twice as powerful. She loathes these deaths which have done her so much harm, one after the other, as if one blow wasn't enough, there had to be two. They have left her so alone, one after the other, as if Anna was so strong she could simply endure it all without flinching. Do her feelings, her tenderheartedness, really count for nothing? Is that any way to treat people?

She'll have to leap over that grave, too, then? All this leaping and prancing about! To tell the truth, she's a little tired now, Anna Lore. The gymnastics these loves require of her are those of an Olympic champion, forever overcoming gigantic hurdles as if they were so many hedges and stakes and fiery hoops. Already as a child she wasn't much good at jumping. She would go horseback riding and was fine when it came to trotting or galloping, but whenever there was an obstacle course where you had to clear fences and banks and water crossings, often as not she would fall, thinking the horse was launched when it had balked, or ready to take to the air when the horse had suddenly decided to veer off round the side. But this time, whether she likes it or feels ready for it or not, she will have to succeed, for there are circumstances in life, albeit very rare, when failure means certain death.

Very well, then, she will gird herself for the fight. And even without Guillaume, even without that body which would protect her from everything, she can perhaps pull it off. Think of all the strength he has given her, day after day, hour after hour, over the past twenty years. Here she is, then, like a helmeted knight at the tournament. And the tournament will be held, of course, in the mountains, where the Great Beings are to be found. That's where she'll be jousting with death. At the thought of the valley, far below, right at the very bottom, that tiny flowering valley called Sorge where she had met Thomas after living there with Guillaume, she laughs: how small it looks! And yet it was there, between the town hall and the marketplace, that she had experienced a storybook romance so tragic that her life was henceforth at stake. Will she be able to climb the great mountainside with its rolling stones all by herself? Of course she will, she has no choice. And once she's up there, assuming she makes it that far, will she be able to harness herself for the fight with long-toothed death? She has no choice. All she has to do is to keep her nerve and be very accurate, forget about the world and empty out her mind and her imagination. Just secure her armor properly, without overlooking a detail, an opening, a fastening; do one thing at a time, calmly, without letting a single memory surface, without letting any of that valley talk intrude, the unfortunate imprecision of which can easily ruin and destroy everything. So Guillaume has left her, has he? She'll give him something to remember her by.

The first third of the ascent is easy. She's in tiptop shape, after all. The meadows are still green and fragrant with their long grass. It's the month of June; so much has happened since the previous August.

Above her, to either side of a split sky, you have the watchful gaze of Jude the Obscure and the eagle eyes of Guillaume which from time to time grow tender again. Both men are present with their great faces observing her as she ascends the flowering path, at once anxious and eager to protect her still, but, as interested parties, unable to assist her in any way. She'll have to fight it out alone. Every now and then she glances up at one of them: the sight of Guillaume's face comforts and sustains her; the sight of Thomas's draws her on. She climbs. Here and there are shepherd's huts, a chapel, a scrap of life still. For the first night, she'll sleep in one of these windowless edifices, where it's cozy and reeks of goat. She contrives to fetch a pail of water, make a fire, tuck a blanket round her and eat some of the rations she's brought along. Guillaume has shown her how to do all this; she mimes the gestures she has seen him perform a hundred times. She has difficulty sleeping, not because she's scared—nothing scares her any more, her plight is far too serious for that—but because she needs love. If only one of them were present—no matter which, either one would do—with his man's love, his tenderness, his wish to protect her. Men when they love a woman are marvelous creatures, it has to be said. No, she can't get to sleep, so she sits on the threshold staring into the night, she's so alone in her ordeal, but thinking of them bucks her up. She thinks of Guillaume on the mountain paths, of his massive hard body, how he was never tired, it was incredible how he was never tired after five hours of rugged ascent, how he was forever picking plants for her or pointing out animal tracks, venturing off along a different path to see where it led, returning, wanting to scale yet another summit on the off chance they might catch a glimpse of a mountain goat. My God, how she loved him. But not quite like a woman, no doubt, more like a wonderstruck child. Then she thinks of Thomas, and of the attention he pays, the patience he shows, when she unwittingly mistreats him with her myriad contradictory emotions. She'd like to have either one sleeping with her; even—why not?—both of them together. One would be in front, the other behind, she'd be snuggled into one man's back with the other tucked in behind her. How happy she'd be, sheathed in that warmth. It's such a shame men can't love a woman two at a time like that without making an issue of it. Then they'd be inseparable, the three of them. You wouldn't have all these problems of divided loyalties, all this agonizing and heartbreak. But when she looks up at their faces in the sky, she sees that neither of them remotely approves of her plan.

Very well, then. Since they are goading her on, she will fight. It'll be too late, afterward, to stand over her body deploring her death, should it come to that. She will have given them fair warning. Both claimed to desire above all else her happiness. Both are honorable men. But happiness for her was to have one in front and one behind, in a rustic bed in a shepherd's hut. There's nothing outlandish about her request. It's simply the wish of a heathen woman, and if they loved her it was because she was a heathen. Why not go one step further? Why stop at these masculine claims to exclusiveness? It's so silly and so bogus, this old-fashioned love where there's just the two of you. They should look at it this way: what couple is happy? They don't wish to? Very well, then, very well. They condemn her to darkness? Good luck to them. But my darling Guillaume, she thinks to herself, isn't it above all my happiness and my delight that you want? Isn't that what you loved in me? And you, my darling Thomas, aren't you entranced by my freedom? It's what you told me, after all. No, no, not at all. They have put on military airs, the pair of them. They're horribly shocked by her proposal. Very well, she'll say no more and will away into the dark night.

The following morning, she climbs higher. It's starting to get arid, with less grass and fewer trees, and no more flowers. But she's still on fairly intimate terms with the gleaming pebbles, she's been through it all a hundred times with Guillaume, you have to climb slowly he was always saying, slow down, slow down, and one day they came across a herd of goats led by a nanny goat, who at the sight of them stopped in her tracks, and they did too. Behind the nanny goat was a sort of secretary goat, who was sent out on reconnaissance. Over she came, stepped up, sniffed them, went back, had a quick exchange with the nanny goat, who without further ado set off once more with her herd. Guillaume and Anna stood without moving as the herd filed past; it was all they could do to refrain from saluting the nanny goat. It's no fun walking on your own. Everything takes longer, and the landscape is less miraculous. Perhaps the mountains weren't so beautiful after all. They were beautiful because Guillaume was there. While she is making her ascent, Thomas is walking through the streets of Bordeaux, lost in thought. As for Guillaume, he's taking a holiday with his family. He's so organized, that man. A wave of suffering has only to hit him, and he instantly reacts—intelligently, actively. It gives Anna something to think about. Once again, it's an example. But an example she's not sure she appreciates all that much. You can't really blame someone for landing on their feet, of course; nothing is more tiresome than melancholics who wallow and splash about in their suffering. Still, it was remarkably swift and businesslike, this turnaround, after only an interval of despair.

IT'S NOT EASY TO move from one body to another. Her old friend Pierre, who was uneasy and critical of her ways, had told Anna as much: you can't just switch beds like that, at the drop of a hat. Perhaps that's where the problem lies, and where a lengthy engagement period comes in handy sometimes. Only then can the body you loved so dearly in the past recede from view, and the new body come forth. But how, in the interval, can you help being both powerfully attached to the past—which lives and quivers inside you still, sings and is comfortable and at home there—and equally powerfully attracted to the new body? Hence the dreadful shilly-shallying that's caused them all so much suffering, Guillaume and Anna and Thomas. Do animals prevaricate like this? Has anyone ever seen a tabby cat or an antelope or a mongoose or a lioness torn between two males—between the memory of happiness with the one and a desire for happiness with the other—muddling them to the point where she no longer knows which one is which or where her own life belongs, wearing herself and her partners out with this incessant back and forth?

On the mountain, she's alone at last and can relax a little. No doubt Guillaume and Thomas will likewise be resting, recharging their batteries. Perhaps, when it comes down to it, she could make do with just the idea of them both? Think of one, think of the other, not get involved or only a tiny bit, just long enough for a microconversation with one and a wave to the other. Sorge could be delightful like that. She would stroll around with a light heart in a sort of perpetual springtime where nothing was ever consummated, forever before the choice, before the fall. Yes, the streets would be broader, there'd be much more air and light in them, the housefronts would be brighter, the sky less unforgiving. When Thomas appeared, there would no longer be a fracture; nor when Guillaume disappeared, an upheaval. She would see them walking by in the same way that she sees friends walking by, familiar faces that no longer have the power to harm you. She would stop loving, stop being consumed by passion, stop blowing up out of all proportion situations that were utterly banal—bumping into someone and falling for them. In her room she would write fairy tales for a change, she would arrange her hair differently and engage in other kinds of relationship with other kinds of people. Her world would no longer be torn apart by passion.

There had been times of late when she was so miserable she would take painkillers, which left her feeling groggy and made reading impossible because the letters would dance before her eyes. The pain of being pulled in two directions was then less acute; she could sleep peacefully, hugging her bolster or pillow to her, even though she now felt as if she were sleeping in a different body, a body heavier and less alive than her own, a body that though still warm felt almost dead. It's funny how the pains of love can burrow so deep into your flesh. It's only love, after all—a fascinating but ultimately secondary aspect of existence. What matters more than anything, surely, is to live, to receive and dispense little joys, to knock together a body of work or a garden bench that will occupy your days; or, if it's families you're fond of, to raise children. That aside, is it really so urgent and so important to form a coruscating bond in life? There were times when Anna was in a hurry to grow old, as her sister who had killed herself had been. To cross to the other side of passion, Japanese-style, on some little footbridge of the soul, to pick three flowers and look up at the sky, to have delicate conversations with the lady next door and pat a passing dog, to forget once and for all the excoriating event of their encounter.

A measure of peace comes over her on finding herself alone at last. She had been alone when she met Guillaume, yet it wasn't a memory she particularly cherished. She had been so outlandishly alone, with no notion of how to engage with others, that at night she would walk the streets of Paris, where she was living at the time, not in the hope of meeting someone—not for anything in the world would she have formed a tie—but simply to be less alone in the world than she was in her mind. Even back then she would walk for hours at a time, striding up and down avenues and boulevards, never once looking into shop windows as she had yet to notice the existence of dresses, but observing people's faces and their way of doing things, no doubt. She would see them in twos—couples—or in threes and fours—friends—chatting, entering a café or exiting a restaurant, and would wonder how they went about meeting, how they went about loving each other or enjoying each other's company. It was all so puzzling to her that she didn't feel at all sad to be alone; she was too busy with her survey, her investigation, even then she was focused on her great task: seeking to understand, amassing clues, examining them, discarding those that led nowhere and conserving anything that might conceal a scrap of information, turning it over and studying it, then setting out again and starting afresh. After a while, she would regularly cross paths with a few others who, like her, lived outside at night: a very sad young man who worked the streets, a flower seller who went from restaurant to restaurant, a battered old lothario in a white convertible. They would give each other a quick wave on their way to their respective employments. It was a hard life, but the data was accumulating, she had less and less need to go out at night, when people's faces and gestures were better lit than during the daytime, and then Guillaume appeared one morning in Sorge, and her life was changed.

For Guillaume, too, had appeared out of nowhere and swept her off her feet (clearly, it's something of a habit with her). All of a sudden he was standing before her in a pair of navy-blue trousers, a detail he would subsequently correct more than once, having never in his life, he maintained, worn navy-blue trousers, and if she fell in love with him it was because he looked as if he had stepped out of a river. His face seemed freshly washed, as did his whole body, albeit clad in a navy-blue suit, and his eyes—or his gaze, rather—seemed to have come straight from a stream. On that occasion, too, she had fallen for him on the spot. You subscribe, then, Anna Lore, to what is usually called love at first sight? Yet, just as one is better off taking hallucinogenic drugs at twenty than at forty, because at twenty there are fewer images moving about inside you than at forty, the surge of emotion she had felt upon meeting Guillaume had been much less unsettling. Something had gushed forth, shooting high into the air and raining down on her existence, but only as the fountains in the gardens of the Palais-Royal do in Paris, broadcasting millions of fine, shimmering particles in the light. Luckily for her she was alone and unattached, so the event could take shape very quickly, very easily, with nothing to stand in its way or hamper its urgent claim to life. There was no time to daydream or conjure up dozens of images; consequently, her love had got off to a very quick start. In no time at all, her solitude had ceased to be an issue, and her past had sunk without a trace; all that remained was an open, luminous and alluring space to go dancing off into.

Heavens, she says to herself as she clambers up her mountain, it was all so long ago, that navy-blue suit and those bright, clear eyes! Not that they were blue, more on the brown side really, but there wasn't a hint of misgiving in them, not a hint of pain or anxiety, they looked on the world and on Anna with confidence and a complete absence of fear, the way you place a beautiful object on a table and that's all there is to it: the beautiful object is there and everything else in the room is forgotten. From the very beginning she had been swept off her feet, captivated, but on that occasion quite painlessly; all that was required of her was to walk on ahead, and with each step the landscape opened out, revealing views she had never seen before, beauties whose existence she would never have suspected. Guillaume was without question the great journey of her life. Henceforth, it was in Guillaume's footsteps that she walked. With each step she would ask herself what Guillaume would have done on this path, where he would have paused for breath or stopped for a bite to eat, in which direction he would have led her. He loved her far too much, Guillaume, and it was this perhaps that was his undoing.

But there on the summit, motionless in his black suit, quietly smoking a cigarette, a bit like a mountain guide awaiting a group of people who wish to be smuggled across the border—isn't that Thomas? Slightly tense, he's standing so that his silhouette can be seen, he's taking a risk, why not? he's perfectly willing to die, he couldn't care less about life, he just wants to do his job properly, there are people to be smuggled over to the other side, including a certain Anna, he'll do what he can, the best he can, and if he messes up ... well, too bad, he'll be sorry, but the occasional fiasco now and then ... He has four packs of cigarettes in his pocket and a jacket that's too thin, he's not the sporting type, he's the type who's always on standby, ready for action, it's what he was trained for, professionally speaking he's rather good at it, and in any case, a person who consents to an emergency and attaches no great value to life always inspires confidence. He can see something stirring in the undergrowth. He doesn't move. At times, he can't see the slightest movement: they've probably turned back for some reason. His orders are to stay there until daybreak, so he'll stay there until daybreak. Something's stirring in a different spot. Two groups? A group that has switched paths? He peels open his second pack of cigarettes, it's starting to feel chilly, he doesn't have enough fond memories to warm him. Never mind.

But no, it's not Thomas, it's a shadow impersonating him. When she gazes up at the summit, sometimes she sees his black suit and slender silhouette, sometimes a form that turns into a cloud, sometimes a tree. When you're walking through a landscape, you see things differently all the time. Heavens, what a mess she has got herself into! Seated against a tree, she thinks of her friends while chewing on a piece of stale bread and cheese. Rima, Christine, Béatrice:

they would have known how to cope! They would have decided on a course of action long ago, and then stuck to it, regardless. What is it she's so scared of losing in choosing one man over the other? Were she to return to Guillaume—dear me, there's probably no chance of that now, too much harm has been done—she would lose that promise of a new life which had so attracted her that she had rushed straight in, her dress flapping about her legs and her hair streaming in the wind. But isn't it an illusion to believe in a new life? Were she to choose Thomas, she would lose a previous life so warm and so tender that it was like being contained in a womb. And yet she had been expelled from that womb, it seems. Can you return to your origins? Not when you've been cast out like Eve, weeping, distraught, covering your face in shame in all those frescoes and paintings.

What now, then? Alone in the big, wide world like a tiny shoot? Heavens, it certainly looks that way, especially as the two men are motionless now, not moving at all, while they await her verdict. Neither of them exerts the slightest pressure any longer, neither of them shows himself, yet they must still be gazing down on her, since whenever she appeals to one of them for a bit of contact, just for a bit of contact, he immediately responds. Some of her more lighthearted friends suggest: a third man? They all burst out laughing, and Anna as well: a third man! Oh no! That's quite enough of that lark! For pity's sake, no more passion! Only one spot on her body has changed since Guillaume left: an eyelid. Ever since he announced he was leaving, that left eyelid has developed a nervous tic, twitching several times a day, then several times an hour—she worries it must be noticeable to others, but no, from what her friends tell her, it appears not.

Still, it's strange that Guillaume didn't do more to get her back. She's baffled by this. He had suffered a terrible blow, of course, when she told him about her passion for Jude the Obscure: but after that? Why did he lend so much credence to her story? Why didn't he just say to himself: I'll place my body between them, I'll lead Anna away, I'll take her on a trip somewhere, move her out of harm's way and get her back? In the past, the moment a tiny thunderstorm appeared on the horizon he would leap into action, with Anna under his arm; nothing, but nothing, could be allowed to jeopardize their great romance. So why hadn't he intervened this time round? Had he immediately thrown in the towel—this man who never gave in? Had he panicked, overwhelmed by the novelty of the situation? Or had he simply grown a little tired of this relationship where there was never a cloud? Were she to question him about this, he would undoubtedly reply, "No, no, it's not that at all." But why had he made so little effort of late? Why had he made so little effort to please her and charm her? Did he think she'd be smitten with him forever? Yet it wasn't like him to rest on his laurels. Impulsive, overflowing with life, Guillaume always wanted to explore new paths, to push on just for the pleasure of advancing and feeling himself at work. What on earth had happened in the secrecy of his soul that he should let go of Anna and allow her to escape? Might there have also been another woman? Or had he, too—since they were so well-aligned that even the most trivial incidents in their lives ran curiously parallel much of the time—found himself at a turning, a crossroads, at precisely the same moment as her? Perhaps he was just desperate to break away? Perhaps things weren't so awful after all?

It would seem, then, that in spite of everything she's now moving in Thomas's direction; Thomas who says nothing and waits. This time, it's not for him to come to her, as he had done on the streets of Sorge, it's for her to go to him, as she had done on the streets of Bordeaux more than a year ago now—searching for him, homing in, circling around his body at a time when she knew almost nothing about him apart from the fact that he reminded her of someone, but whom? She's made progress over the past year. She knows now that he's not Jude the Obscure, not the watchmaker who sells hourglasses and water clocks in the rue Gay-Lussac, not the murdered Russian poet familiar to us from black and white photos, and certainly not that vigilante cowboy who turns up on the edge of town in the Wild West. He's not in a film, he's not in a novel, and he can't really be said to be in a painting either. She seems to have emerged from the realm of fiction at last.

BUT WILL SHE STILL love him, outside the realm of fiction? She recalls certain facial expressions she had found astonishing in bed; they didn't belong to Jude the Obscure at all, and she had found it hard to decide whether she liked them or not. This incursion of an unknown Thomas had scared her slightly: might he be a total stranger? Someone who had nothing in common with her whatsoever? But she comforts herself with the thought that, on her very first night with Guillaume, she had been astounded—again, in bed—to discover he had a left profile she had never seen before and would never have suspected. Even then she had wondered: will I be able to love him with this profile I've never seen before, which is certainly not unbecoming but is wholly alien to everything that led me to fall in love with him? And then she had got used to his left profile, had ceased noticing it as something unfamiliar, and before long it had become so much part of Guillaume that she never again viewed it as something alien and apart from him, but, on the contrary, as an additional clue to his person, his wishes, his heart.

Will she love the real Thomas? For the moment, he's canny enough, cunning enough even—without meaning to be and without knowing it—to mould himself to her desires. At all times, that is, he retains something of Jude the Obscure. It may be that the desire someone feels for you moulds you in its shape, and that a woman who falls in love with a cowboy brings out the cowboy in a man who is nothing of the kind. She notes in him, as they walk through the streets of Bordeaux he wants to show her, a distinct caution and reserve. But he was already like that in Sorge: cautious and reserved. He really is that way, then. She is the one who exclaims, announces, decides, declares; he enters her dream as best he can and never says no. When they stop for lunch, for example, in a windswept square, he's so reserved that he might as well be Jude the Obscure, were it not for the fact that he's Thomas. Yes, that's it, that's exactly it: during all these months of preparation, he has been bent on entering her dream and adopting its forms.

And that's a sign of love, no? Or of a wish to win her heart, at least. Thomas is self-effacing, miming what he sees reflected in Anna's eyes so as to become what she desires. He might even enjoy doing so; enjoy it more than anything, in fact—not as a general rule, but when he's in love, as he was at seventeen and then a second time at thirty. Twice he fell madly in love and twice it didn't work out. The first time, it's safe to assume, he was young and unexperienced, and who hasn't had the experience of being denied a body they loved but had no idea how to reach. The second time he was more mature, but the blow was so powerful, the apparition so spellbinding, that he lost all consciousness of it. Today, he's not so young as he was, and he has Anna before him, reminding him of these two women from his past, and this time he's not going to mess up. If he messes up, that's his lot as far as love's concerned. He'll call it quits, and perhaps be none the worse for it; still, he'll fall asleep one day with the idea that he has failed in love. For Anna, then, it's worth bringing all his skills to bear: everything he has seen, thought, read, listened to, and understood over the past fifty years. Everything he has experienced, suffered, endured, hoped for, believed, imagined, and dreamed in the last fifty years. While she's lunching with him on that windswept square in Bordeaux, all this is present inside him, it's all been brought into play. And if he has such a powerful effect on her, it's perhaps because a presence as complete as this is something of a rarity all the same.

That's how he wins her over. Because welling up inside him is his whole life, convened and gathered together just for her. Just so he can possess her. It makes for an odd character, more like an animal tamer alone with a wild beast or an artist bent over his work than a man in love. She could perfectly well flee, Anna. She can see it's not Jude the Obscure; though, come to think of it, isn't this how Jude the Obscure behaved when he was in love? No matter! She could flee, she could call a halt right now to this man and Bordeaux, whose streets are a bit too sunny at times and bore her, but she's moved by his hidden intensity and the unspoken way in which he has staked his all. Not for a second does she imagine that she plays any part in this—she, Anna. She has never really believed in love. She's simply a charming woman quite beside herself with desire. It so happens, though, that for this charming woman whose desire has such a powerful effect on him, a man performs an extraordinary operation, gathering his entire life together just to keep her beside him. She has always liked people who slave away at things. She likes it when they go to great lengths to realize their full potential in the execution of some colossal task, like Guillaume scaling some incredible peak. She has perhaps done this herself, in order to survive. So she watches Thomas making this considerable effort to convene his entire life and all of his dreams—without moving a finger, without batting an eyelid—while they stroll about, sit at a table together eating carpaccio, thumb through a book or two at a flea market, or admire a beautiful door in the street. It gives her food for thought and it moves her.

Yes, it's this, no doubt, that she likes: this slim, taut presence; and the silence of that presence, because when you're on a tightrope high in the air you don't talk much. You not only have to concentrate but to put yourself in a frame of mind where you're remote from everything and at the same time more alive to the world than ever before. He moves like a blade through the streets of Bordeaux, showing her the ones he walks along when alone and lost in thought. In these huge and at times quite deserted blond avenues, where marvelous eighteenth-century buildings of unparalleled grace answer one another as if in a mirror, he walks steadily on, neither hopeful nor afraid, just doing his job as a man as best he can. From time to time, he peers at her quizzically; like all men, he wants to buy her sweets and trinkets, anything that will give her pleasure; sometimes a question flares up inside him, he stops, asks her in a voice that's a tiny bit different from his usual voice, less composed, more like an exclamation: "But Anna, tell me . . . ," but he's forgotten what it was he wanted to ask, and she answers yes. The yes reassures him for a moment, then unsettles him again, for no one really knows to what question the yes is a response. Still, it's a clue of sorts just the same. He stops and peers gravely at her; yes, she says. Yes? he resumes. And sometimes these are their only conversations.

He's scarcely more relaxed in bed, not quite sure how to act since he hasn't got a clue what's going on. She laughs, she puts him at ease, he laughs too and for a moment sheds all the tension gathered inside him, the gaping question his life has become whenever he thinks of Anna or is with her. She, too, is surprised to find herself with a different body, a different form of nakedness than the one she's accustomed to. That's why they contemplate each other with astonishment and a faint but very real sense of dread, pretending to act like conventional lovers, but it's as if the room has been turned upside down, the building overturned, the town tipped over, the world disarranged and then rearranged differently, the rivers are flowing in the wrong directions, there's a desert in place of the Garonne and an ocean advancing where there used to be the local park, everything has changed, she says, yes he replies. And when they emerge from this timid and somewhat fearful contact, where it does indeed seem to be out beyond their bodies that something is happening and has happened, they're still surprised to have dared to touch one another, to have actually touched one another, as if in reality this had to be something impossible, something quite simply unthinkable.

Guillaume is fading from her mind. She feels ashamed to be forgetting him, ashamed to no longer quite recall the shape of their love. She tries desperately to recover it the way you assemble objects and photos and letters in order to conjure up the past once more. At times she feels like one of those people an entire chapter of whose life has simply vanished; at others, the memory of Guillaume and of their love for each other—of the very shape and beating heart of that love—rises up with such force that Thomas appears like a complete stranger all of a sudden: a terrifying illusion, a colossal misunderstanding, a dead end, a gaping hole in her existence. And Anna, who only a minute before had been gazing fondly at Thomas and talking to him in what she had assumed to be a state of perfect understanding, looks on him as a ghost who has run off with her man, a wraith who has devoured her beloved, an evil spirit who has left her naked and alone in the world. But the reconciliations are less arduous than a few months back. Thomas has only to make a gesture or say a word while looking away and she edges that tiny bit closer to him, he weighs as little as possible, he's so unobtrusive that she even has room to move slightly, she glances round at him again and he pretends not to notice, to take nothing in, with a genius for self-effacement Anna finds impressive and is grateful for.

It's done, she's back together with him, though it's nothing to write home about and they'll both pretend to know nothing of the matter. For the conditions governing the ebb and flow of Anna's moods are so imponderable that simply moving a chair or batting an eyelid can sometimes lead to a whirlpool forming. Basically, they dance a sort of pavane in which their eyes don't meet, pretending to gaze into the distance and only brushing against each other by accident; but when all of a sudden their eyes do meet, as is bound to happen, the question is less harrowing henceforth for Thomas—and the tension on both sides less rapt—than when they were walking by that nondescript river all that time ago, telling each other love stories without once touching. When their eyes meet, they say yes to each other. Then they change the subject.

She's no longer in love with Guillaume. He has abandoned her. Had he wished to go on loving her, wished to go on being loved by her, he should have stayed where he was and stood his ground; it wasn't *that* difficult, for heaven's sake. He had only to think of their sailboat, the *Virginia*, which they had packed with a fortnight's supplies for a trip along the coast. The night before, they had slept in a hotel on the beach, the terrace of their room overrun with great clusters of purple, violet and pink blossoms, and at dusk he'd gone for a walk on the sand. She had stayed behind in the room, worn out by love, but had gone out onto the balcony to watch him from behind the flowers. Later on, she had gone to join him, and making their way over the rocks at the water's edge they'd ended up dining at a deserted crossroads, where a solitary cat crossed back and forth, glancing round each time before advancing, keeping an eye out for oncoming cars. They'd seen pink flamingos. They'd seen swarms of bees. They'd seen gray breakers come crashing down on them from a heavy sea. They'd seen a gale in a harbor where Guillaume flailed about naked on the bridge. They'd seen turquoise waters that were too cold for Anna. They'd seen so many things together that her mind was like an attic filled with a thousand objects. Why had he emptied out that attic, which one day would look like a deserted hall? Nothing is odder than an empty, tidy attic. There was an attic like that at her grandparents' home, a huge house near Béziers, in the vineyards. Nobody liked going there.

They'd seen wild boar roaming through their garden at dusk. They'd seen mountain goats right at the very top of a mountain. They'd seen a hundred hotel rooms and a hundred towns and villages. They'd seen each other drained, cheerful, famished, inquisitive, on edge. They'd seen donkeys courting beneath an apple tree. They'd seen at least ten parks and twenty châteaus and been equally bored by them all. They'd seen an owl on their window ledge. They'd seen friends, though not too often as they liked to keep to themselves. They'd seen jewelry he'd bought for her, which annoyed Anna, who disliked jewelry. They'd seen thousands of roads, and each time Guillaume was amazed more importance wasn't attached to roads in films. They'd listened to music in the car, and sometimes she had wept it was so beautiful and she was so happy with him. They'd visited cathedrals and caves. They'd walked through forests with orange butterflies leading the way. They'd read books, though she didn't read much when she was next to him because she was too busy looking at him. They'd taken a hundred baths together, when he washed her hair. They'd slept for thousands of nights together, she loved his scent, his hands, his gaze, and was always the first to tire; not him. They'd seen dawns and nights. They'd shared three houses in Sorge before settling into the last and biggest of the three. They'd owned a bird and a cat, and she'd have liked to have owned a goat. They had lived solely together, and in his fury he wanted to empty out that attic and fling their entire life through the skylights in the roof, along with all the love they had shared. Good luck to him. From now on, she would love Thomas and put together a new attic of images.

HOW STRANGE IT IS to leave someone you love for someone you love. You cross a footbridge that has no name, that's not named in any poem. Nowhere is a name given to this footbridge, which is why Anna finds it so difficult to cross. She's just beginning to tell Thomas and Guillaume apart. Fortunately, they don't have at all the same body language; in bed they are very different. It's in bed, in fact, that the difference is most pronounced. It's very restful, therefore, in bed, for Thomas at that point is no longer Guillaume. And, little by little, Anna's body takes leave of Guillaume to go and join Thomas. But wasn't that what it was all about from the beginning? Wasn't that why Guillaume had broken with her so swiftly and so harshly? Anna's shrink had told her as much even before anything had actually happened: "It's very erotic, this relationship with Thomas." "You think so? Erotic?" All they had done was talk. "Yes, but what a conversation!" she said. "What do you mean, 'what a conversation!'?" Had they once touched on matters intimate, confidential, private? Not at all. They talked solely about books, people in Sorge, and what they were up to at the time. "It's as though we were panting," Anna told the shrink. "Not in a million years would I have touched on anything sexual with this buttoned-up man, not in a million years.... But it was as if we were breathing a bit too heavily for a normal conversation." And she remembered how you could make love with words, how it can even be the most powerful way of all. In the cafés of Sorge, Thomas and she had been in bed together each morning—without ever touching on the matter, seated side by side at their café table, gazing into the distance. But their words were so entangled, so beautifully entwined, they moved so well together.... And Guillaume, it was incredible, Guillaume had sensed this, had understood. Hence his brutal, horrifying response. "Thomas, would you say we were making love when we sat on a café terrace chatting about books and what we were up to and people in Sorge?" "Maybe," he says. "You made a curious impression on me. I would try to escape, the next day I'd go for lunch in Tauge or Venves, I would try to distance myself from you, I couldn't stop thinking about you, I couldn't understand a thing." "Did your sex start playing up at all?" she asks. "No, my sex was fine," he says, "it was my heart that was feeling battered and apprehensive, scared. I couldn't understand what was going on. I had given up on love—I swear to you, I genuinely wanted no more love. I saw myself leading a quiet life characterized by friendships and serenity, and a kind of melancholy I'd grown rather fond of. I never thought for a second of love when I saw you. I thought to myself, well, that was a pleasant encounter, an interesting conversation; but then later I found myself thinking far too much about you. Not about your body, not a bit, I swear to you, and I apologize for that. No, I would think of talking to you and how enjoyable it was and how I'd have loved to talk to you all the time." "But you were in love with me just the same, Thomas, weren't you?" "No, not at all," he says. "I wasn't in love with you—at least, I didn't think of you in those terms. I'd wake up in the morning feeling cheerful at the idea I might run into you in Sorge, in which case we would have a good conversation, you would say things I found interesting, I would tell you what I thought of them, you would disagree and take issue with me, and I would then have to find new arguments, all of which made for a much more interesting summer than usual."

As in one of those science-fiction movies where the walls protecting a secret cavern (at the center of which an entire population is preparing a new world) part for a moment to admit an aircraft carrier or let out a spaceship, enormous slow movements are taking place inside Anna. Walls you would have thought fixed pivot and change place, rocks that had seemed heavy and immovable slide away like cardboard boulders being shunted back and forth on a stage set. Never before has she witnessed a transformation on quite such a scale. It's most peculiar. Perhaps in the end it was this, rather than some alarming, madcap decision, that her old friend Pierre had always been on the lookout for. Never in her life has she talked so much to friends about what's going on inside her. Whether she bumps into Brigitte, Delphine, Sophie, Gilles, Jacques, Jacques's girlfriend, Sophie's sister, or Gilles's mother, to the question "How are you?" she immediately responds by relating in detail, for each day of each month, the advance of the transformation taking place—the tremors, the doubts, the convictions, the expectations. The whole world knows about her odyssey, everyone takes a passionate interest in it. "It's possible, then?" asks Brigitte, goggle-eyed, before telling Anna how she would love to be alone, love to be free enough one day, to be consumed by passion like never before, she wants to know how it feels to be driven out of your mind by passion and whether the following day your mind is a complete blank. Maria has been following the revolution closely. From the very beginning she has had an idea of how it will end, and the idea looks promising, but she doesn't want to share it with Anna, she says, for fear it might influence her. Gilles, who had all but stopped phoning, now calls her regularly: What's new? How's it going? Jacques recommends books, Marceline keeps her informed about events in Bordeaux. Everybody talks about Thomas and Guillaume in the first person, as if Thomas and Guillaume were now household names whose destinies everybody was following at the same time as Anna's.

And, deep down, this is what Anna Lore has always dreamed of. Not that she wants to make an exhibition of herself, the expression used by her elderly father, who, for the first time in her life, she has also confided in, and who, as a stickler for discretion, is worried she might go too far, might talk too much and give herself a bad name. No, what she has always dreamed of is having the world's backing, of being buoyed up and carried along by a lovable and loving throng of people while she carves out a difficult and fascinating path. How precious it is, not to be alone in the streets of Bordeaux where her love is hiding. To have around her this stream of benign and friendly presences so interested in her adventure that you would think it was doing them good, too. Anna, for her part, has never shown much interest in the love lives of others, but then it's not often that they talk about them, or only in passing. Sometimes she scans their faces or their tone of voice for a lassitude, a more than justified wish to talk about something else for a change—their own lives, for example. But no, however carefully she scrutinizes their faces or listens to the sounds of their words, all she sees and hears is a wish to participate in her great adventure. And depending on what she is narrating and how she narrates it in the fullness of time, their views will espouse her own, forming a curve when she describes a curve, straightening up when she straightens up, sinking down with her when she descends into a dark spot, buoying her up when she's buoyant. It's thanks to this stream of people that she can advance; alone, she might not manage it.

It was at this point that Anna heard about the delinquent from Kiev for the first time. It was on television, she was looking at pictures of her on the screen, and the delinquent from Kiev might have been her own sister, it was incredible. The girl, who was younger and skinnier than Anna but whose eyes were very similar to her own, her mouth, too, and the shape of her face, her shoulders even, had just murdered her two lovers. Anna began following daily, almost hourly, the story of the delinquent from Kiev, who some news media also referred to as the teenager from Kiev, though the girl was over twenty (but looked a lot younger at times, it's true). She'd had two lovers, Oleg and Micha, who were brothers. She had begun by having an affair with Micha; they had even had a child, who died in infancy. As a result of that bereavement, it seems, the girl from Kiev became very unhappy and fell into a sort of depression; Micha did what he could to help her, but she had begun to behave rather erratically, going out late to bars, drinking too much and not coming home at night. Micha would go looking for her in Kiev around three or four in the morning, people would tell him she had gone this way or that way, he would retrace her steps and sometimes wouldn't find her. Micha was thirty, Oleg twenty-six. For some unknown reason, since she had never shown the slightest interest in him, Evangeline—that was the girl's name—would often seek refuge at Oleg's. He had always found her rather attractive, but would never have thought of touching her since she belonged to his brother, and he liked his brother. But Evangeline seemed to be so lost, so unhinged by the death of her baby, and to find Oleg's presence so comforting, that what was bound to happen happened: one night they slept together, he was very moved by her and a sort of "family lie" was born.

Oleg and Micha, of course, used to meet and talk. Micha would mention his concerns about Evangeline's health and conduct to his brother; Oleg, meanwhile, couldn't bring himself to tell Micha that Evangeline was sleeping with him. But she was also sleeping with Micha, since she was sharing herself between the two brothers, and it was this sharing, it seems, that was doing her some good, helping her get back on her feet. Things got horribly out of hand, however, because she was as crazy about Micha as she was about Oleg; above all, in proportion as the lie grew and took root between them, her love for the two brothers also grew, until it had become an irrepressible erotic need. She would rush over to Micha's to sleep with him, and once the deed was done, quickly get dressed and rush back to Oleg's. The pain caused by the loss of her baby subsided. Rushing back and forth like this from one street and apartment to the other, one man to the other, one bed to the other, comforted her a little. Micha and Oleg thought her distinctly loopy; her passion struck them as exorbitant and dysfunctional, and they both found it almost embarrassing. But the sight of a pair of imploring eyes and a compliant, sylphlike body fretfully offering itself to you is always pleasing to a man. And so they took advantage of the situation, as any man would have done.

Day in, day out, Anna followed the story of the delinquent from Kiev, which all the television channels and radio stations were talking about; it was such a pretty tale and, what with the murders, so romantic that everyone was fascinated by it. Televised debates were held with psychoanalysts and philosophers, Ukraine specialists, legal experts: all relished the opportunity—who can blame them?—of investigating the case of the delinquent from Kiev. You saw photos of her at six, at eight, journalists tracked down her old schoolteachers who explained what a sweet little girl she was, they interviewed her father (still reeling from the shock) and university friends who explained that she'd wanted to be a writer. She had killed the two brothers with a dagger, and when you saw her on the day of her arrest she seemed perfectly calm and composed, she even looked rather distinguished. What had happened? In a press conference that was shared over and over on the internet and already had ten million clicks, she calmly explained, as if discussing a novel she had written, that there had come a moment when, weary of being unable to choose between the two lovers whom she desired equally with a tender, fiery passion, she had thought of taking her own life, but had dismissed the idea because she had no wish to die. Then, little by little, the idea of killing one of her lovers had occurred to her. At the beginning, it was just one or the other. But which one? She thought of murder as something enjoyable, yes, she admits this, and why not? there was no point beating about the bush. Yes, she had thought killing one of them might do her some good. At the same time, it seemed a shame to end up either without Micha or without Oleg. To end up with either Micha or Oleg. It seemed a shame to have to choose, since choosing was the one thing she was incapable of doing.

Each morning, Anna would switch the television or her computer on. Evangeline was still there, increasingly calm and composed as the days went by since the two murders. One afternoon, she couldn't stand it any longer, she told the journalists, while calmly adjusting a bracelet on her wrist. She wondered if she had a dagger at home, like a character in a novel. No, of course she didn't have a dagger, no one owns a dagger in this day and age. But what was quite extraordinary was that both men had offered her a rather stylish switchblade at the start of their relationship. The one Micha had given her had an ivory handle; the one from Oleg had a handle made of horn. Apart from that, the knives were the same model and make, with a lion's head stamped into the blade. Micha's was a bit slimmer than Oleg's; a "lady's knife," whereas Oleg's was a man's. Basically, Evangeline calmly explained, she had always wanted to kill. She wasn't obsessed with the idea of murder, it wasn't that, she wasn't a psychopath, but it was true that whenever she thought of something desperate that might really content her, it wasn't erotic pleasures that came to mind, which were very enjoyable, of course, but lacked the intensity she had in her. No, she had always longed to commit a murder, she was certain of that. Until now, she had refrained from doing so, because it's not done. She could have gone on refraining, and still be refraining to this day, had she not lost the baby, but the loss of that baby had opened a possibility.

"I took my two knives," she explained, "first I went to Micha's, his chest was broad, his shirt white, I stripped naked to sleep with him, then I went over to my bag where the little white dagger with the ivory handle was, went back to him and thrust it into his heart, at the exact spot where he loved me." Silence in the hall where the press conference was being held. An Italian journalist held up a finger. "Did he suffer?" "I don't know," replied Evangeline; "no, I don't think so, he collapsed on the spot." An English journalist from the *Times* raised a finger, she was wearing a pretty, close-fitting, gray dress and had a

Forties-style haircut: "Did he scream?" she asked in English. "No," said Evangeline, "he looked surprised, that's all." "How does it feel to kill a man?" asked a little journalist from the south of France. For a moment Evangeline didn't say anything. They thought she wasn't going to answer, was going to duck the question; but no, after a few minutes, she replied. "You don't feel anything," she said. "Nothing really." It's unbelievable that she's being filmed recounting in all earnestness the murders she has committed, thought Anna. It must be the first time this has ever happened. We live in a terrifying world where you can explain at a press conference why and how you killed people. As if you were talking about a film or a book. And then she gave up on Evangeline and Kiev.

She's seeing Thomas, she's seeing more and more of Thomas, who secretly comes to Sorge while Guillaume has gone to stay with friends by the sea. It feels very odd to have Thomas in the house she has lived in with Guillaume. To begin with, it's very strange, then after a while she gets used to it. The more he visits, the more he drives out Guillaume. He hangs his tweed jacket on a coat hook in the hall, something Guillaume never did; Guillaume, moreover, didn't wear tweed jackets, so she takes a liking to this tweed jacket that doesn't remind her of anything. There's another thing, too, that makes a welcome difference: Guillaume used to touch her all the time. Wherever she went, whatever she might happen to be doing, Guillaume's hand would touch her body, continually, whereas Thomas never touches her without warning—never. He only touches her if she has touched him first. And when he does touch her, it's never as fiery or as brutal as hers is, it's less hurried and more restrained, and that's how he drives Guillaume from the house. They sleep in the bed she used to sleep in with Guillaume, at the beginning she had told herself she would buy another bed or move the bedroom elsewhere in the house, but a bed is a bed, a bedroom a bedroom and made for love, it would feel forced switching everything around like that, so she keeps the bedroom and she keeps the bed, and she just endeavors never to mistake Thomas for Guillaume.

For a long time she feels awkward, very ill at ease even, when going about her usual rituals in his presence—at bedtime or at breakfast, in the bathroom, during evenings by the fire. But how can you change these things? her friends ask: you are who you are, it's not because a new man has turned up that you're suddenly going to turn into someone else. Yes, no doubt, but whenever she's very happy with Thomas it's because he's doing something or saying something distinctly different from Guillaume. He has adopted a room, for example, that Guillaume had hardly ever set foot in. She hadn't pointed it out to him, he had found it all by himself. It's in this room that makes phone calls or sits himself down at a table when he has something he needs to write, and whereas before he came along it had vaguely served as a kind of laundry room, its tall cupboards heaped with linen, it's now used by him as a kind of office which he always asks her permission before entering, for never in her home does he act as if he owns the place; and while he's writing at the table and she comes over and places her hand on his shoulder—gently, ever so gently, because before Anna came along he didn't much like being touched on the shoulder either—she gazes out through the oval window in the side of the roof and sees a marvelous garden, her own garden as she's never really seen it before, having never looked at it through that window, and the long blades of very pale green grass which she can make out in the distance, the tiny gate, the dreamy blue cabbages that a gardener from time to time comes to water, or to dig up perhaps—she wouldn't know, she's not at all interested in gardening—form a very beautiful landscape, she feels.

Her stomach doesn't hurt as much as it did at the beginning, she's growing slimmer and darker, and a thing she finds increasingly attractive about

Thomas is that he lets her come to him. He doesn't move. The man has a real gift for presence, distance. He always stands a few yards back, never right up against her unless she has come up to him first, never cuddling up to her unless she has cuddled up to him first, and even then, though extremely responsive, he doesn't move. She marvels at this, for Guillaume would devour her all the time, and being devoured nonstop like that could be very tiring at times. Basically, Thomas could be with her all the time and yet remain indefinitely a stranger, forever present but forever with an air of Jude the Obscure about him; could touch her without touching her, bed her without bedding her, kiss her without either of them being quite sure their lips and mouths had actually met. He leaves a bit of fiction between them, as if the whole thing had been dreamed up perhaps; and yet, wherever she turns, he's there, like a symbol on a page: you can circle round it to your heart's content, but your eyes are always drawn back to this symbol which signifies something in a language you have yet to decipher.

They only go out after dark, since she's adamant that, for the time being, no one must know they're together. It's not that she's anxious about her reputation, she just doesn't want somebody telling Guillaume they have seen her with Thomas and hurting him. Thomas understands and accepts this. And it's not such a bad thing, this provisional secrecy, since they only go out at night under an open sky, and a sky so gigantic—and they themselves so gray in the gloom, like shadows—that it makes these first steps of their life together rather magical. They walk down roads hand in hand, not a single car goes by, the tall trees are still, their footsteps ring on the asphalt. They chat and laugh, she picks a few gray flowers, they make their way down to a still lake. Sometimes he grumbles a bit, saying he's tired of all this secrecy, that he's looking forward to having Anna with him during the daytime, in broad daylight, that he doesn't like secrecy, that it makes him uneasy, that it's not his style. She understands, she recognizes this, but asks him to hang on for a few weeks longer, the time it takes for Guillaume to recover fully and stop hurting. Out of masculine solidarity, but also because there is no alternative, Thomas goes along with her, acknowledging, "Yes, you're right...." Invariably, though, as if he had grown forgetful of Anna's wishes, some chance event gives him the opportunity to bump into her in the daytime, in broad daylight, leaving her with no alternative but to walk up to him in broad daylight. "You're going too far," she says. "I know," he says. And continually present between them is that urgent need felt on the very first day, during the very first coffee taken together in Sorge: the need to be together, always, incessantly, as if it had become quite impossible to tell their bodies apart.

Never before had she felt such a need to be with someone, to be pressed up against someone, continually. Even with Guillaume, whom she had loved deeply, she hadn't wanted such a union. True, it had been marvelous to be living together, but what had been still more marvelous was when they went outdoors on those extraordinary hikes—outdoors precisely. It was there that they came together best: outdoors, on the mule tracks, during the ascent, in the mountains. It wasn't exactly home. With Thomas, yes, she would like to get married, there's no other word for it. And one day, when she had told him this: "Well, I'll marry you in that case," he said. For him, there was no real need, he had already been married and hadn't found it terribly fulfilling. But if that was what Anna wanted, it was fine by him. She doesn't really know how you go about marrying someone, having never wished to get married before. Thomas mentions practical matters. No, no, it's not practical matters Anna is interested in, she couldn't care less about practical matters, what she wants is a secret, mystic ceremony, a rite of passage in which you forsake your past in order to embark on a new life, in the same way that Marie-Antoinette, when she was led to Louis XVI, had to pass through a pavilion where she was disrobed, stripped bare, made to leave all her past possessions and friends behind and dress up differently, and then emerged from the pavilion by another door to go toward her new life. "There you have it," said Anna to Thomas, "that's what I want, that's exactly what I want."

He understands, for he has begun to understand everything Anna thinks, everything she wants and is. He never says no to her, except on days when she wants secrecy. For secrecy, it's no. For that, and for that alone, it's no. And when, in an attempt to cajole him, to enchant and disarm him, she says: "I've always been rather secretive, you know, it's my world, I feel perfectly at home there"—"No," he says, "it's out of the question." On this issue of secrecy, he won't budge. It's the one question on which he will not budge. "We could carry on an affair and see each other in secret," she says, taking advantage of moments when he's watching her undress, "it might even be more exciting that way." "No," he says. And she loves coming up against this rock, of course. It's the one cause he never fails to defend; in everything else he's a model of delicacy and discretion. He would like her to meet his sons. She bridles at this. What has their love got to do with his two sons? What business is it of theirs? It *is* their business, he replies calmly. Children need to know what sort of life their father is leading, and with whom. He's so proud, she thinks, to have a girlfriend younger than himself and still pretty that he wants to show her off like a trophy, and she tells him so. "Not at all," he replies, laughing, "I happen to love you, and you're important to me. I'm very fond of my children. If I was just having a fling, I wouldn't mention it, but my life is changing because of you, I owe it to myself to show them how, and why, and by whom, my life has been changed."

She thinks long and hard about the soundness of such a view. She suspects him of wanting to prove what a man he is. At the same time, it makes her smile, she finds it moving. She suspects him of wanting to prove to his children and friends how exceptional he is, since he's capable of seducing a younger woman, and she doesn't want any part of that. What does he want to show her off for? She doesn't take at all kindly to being used as a foil. What she had always liked about Guillaume was that they saw no one when they were together. She was his own private marvel, nobody else's. Guillaume had no need to show her off; that was his great strength. So she studies Thomas from that angle. She wants to be quite sure that, were they living together in the wilderness, he would be happy in the wilderness with her. Yes, he says, but we're not living in the wilderness. What's more, she herself, she suspects, is no longer all that fond of secrecy. The people of Sorges had known, of course, that she and Guillaume lived together, but since they did very little entertaining because they traveled a lot and each had their own group of friends, and since he seldom accompanied her to Paris, it had been like living in the back of a cave. She liked that, Anna Lore. In her wallet she kept a photo of Guillaume which she would sometimes show to friends in Paris, but it was all they really knew of him: this face from twenty years ago that no longer bore much resemblance to him.

Sometimes when she's gazing out of the window with nothing much to occupy her, she wonders if she hasn't fallen in love with Jude the Obscure in order to be done with secrecy. It's a vast, bottomless question that touches on regions of her being she may not wish to examine more closely. She has no desire to know why she has always been so fond of secrecy. And it's odd that in Anna Lore, who always wants to know everything and always does her best to understand, there should be this point she has no wish to explore. Might something terrifying be lurking there? No, of course not; and in any case, terrifying things don't terrify her. No, it's more a feeling she has that, were that armor-plating to be removed, her body would be so exposed that it would suffer harm. She's prudent and sensible, therefore, rather than lily-livered or fearful. But from now on, whenever she hears the word secrecy, whenever someone mentions the word secrecy in her presence, she thinks of Jude the Obscure looming up on the streets of Sorge, and of how that apparition had turned things inside out, revealing the true face of secrecy rather than its underside, where she had always lived.

The more Thomas-Jude puts on bodily form, the less desultory her passion becomes and the more she recovers of her former calm. One day, no doubt, she will love him as she had loved Guillaume, with a sort of quiet, untroubled joy. And no doubt he will always light up that side of her—or if not always, for a long time to come—as though concealed therein was a long buried electrical circuit along which the current would begin to flow the moment she set eyes on him. But there are also times when a huge weariness comes over her at the thought of all this love, this whole momentous affair, a lassitude so great that all that is left for her is to fling herself down on a bed or a couch or a sofa and, closing her eyes, ask herself if the whole thing isn't entirely her own invention.

SHE WOULD LIKE TO draw things out a little longer. Guillaume, of course, has left her, and she's now secretly with Thomas, but one of the nice things about secrecy is that you can do an about-face all of a sudden. And so she buys time, though at the risk of trying his patience. Thomas is willing to play along, but not for very long. The moment she gives up the struggle, the moment she lets up, he once again raises the possibility of a daytime existence. She pretends not to understand, finds an excuse for staying in the shadows, at which point he, too, pulls an apartment from his pocket, though for quite the opposite reason to Guillaume, who, in taking her to visit the seaside apartment he had bought, not so that they could live there but so that they could live more comfortably in Sorge, had burned his bridges. Thomas, too, then, has bought an apartment. With high ceilings because she had told him one day that she dreamed of high ceilings like those in her grandmother's apartment in Brussels, where, to a child lying in bed at night, the ceiling seemed so high that even the bulkier items of furniture looked tiny. She had also told him, feckless creature that she was, that she liked fireplaces and odd corners in a house. It hadn't taken him long, he had found it all in double quick time—the high windows, the fireplaces, the nooks, the stairs—and Anna, upon hearing this, had bolted like a hare. Come back, come back, he pleaded in his emails, for once again she wanted to break off the relationship. She couldn't do it, he had overstepped the mark in offering her the apartment Guillaume had refused her, in imagining she would spend more than a minute there, in welcoming her into his life—she, who had no wish to be welcomed anywhere, just to carry on playing fast and loose with love! Enough was enough.

Yet, though they had broken off in tears and grief, she began dreaming of the apartment. Just a tiny bit. She wouldn't have permitted herself to dream of it for more than a few minutes. But it was there in her daydreams now, fastened to Thomas's silhouette, she imagined the windows and thought of her grandmother, whose presence she had always liked, she wondered if the windows had espagnolettes. She opened them, closed them again, then glanced round at Thomas who was standing behind her in the room, and said: "It's dusk" or "It's windy out this evening." He had mentioned the neighborhood the apartment was in and had even told her the name of the street. She could see exactly which street it was, with its small, crescent-shaped square and a fountain on the rim of which they had sat to eat ice cream one day when she was in Bordeaux. She could even see which building it was, for they had remarked on it. At home in Sorge, estranged from Thomas but from Guillaume as well, alone these past few days and at peace with herself for once, she gazes up at the windows of the apartment. She's still seated on the rim of the fountain, her back's a bit sore from the cold stone, Thomas isn't there, she's eating an ice cream, watching people go by—lovers with their arms round each other's waist, boys on bicycles—and gazing up at the windows, wondering if she'll ever manage to live with Thomas.

He had been far too impetuous, thrusting an apartment on her like that when he knew full well how she was always wriggling out of things. A token of love? Yes, without a doubt, but Anna had no time for the kind of love that wants to seize hold of you and place you under house arrest—surely he had understood that? "You'll just be spending a few days here from time to time," he had told her, "we'll be better off here than back at my apartment with my son or in a hotel." Yes. But whether she comes here or not, or very little, it will still be their apartment, an apartment intended and acquired for them, as a couple. Would she be forming a couple with Thomas, then? No, of course she wouldn't, you can't live with Jude the Obscure. At a pinch you can marry him in a ceremony that exists in a kind of novel, but you can't share an apartment with him, even a high-ceilinged one, in a street with a name, near a square with another name, the whole thing forming a postal address where people can write to you, that you have to register. But the empty apartment awaiting them has turned into the center of Bordeaux, of course. They get back in touch because she can no longer live without Thomas, but no mention is made of the apartment. She returns to Bordeaux, they stroll around, by chance end up in the same street and sit down beside the fountain once more; they pay no attention to the building in front of them. "You went a bit far," she tells him. "Yes, I'm sorry about that," he says. But at no point does he say he has given up on the apartment.

He takes her to another house he used to live in, at present inhabited by friends who are away on vacation. She enters the house the way a cat comes in from a downpour, raising a paw, leaving it hanging in the air for a second, looking around for a dry patch, and only then, after failing to find one, advancing with a mixture of revulsion and curiosity in the presence of these new sensations. It's odd to be entering a house where Thomas Lenz has had so many experiences, but what's even odder, and a good sign, is that he moves about there with the same self-restraint, the same absence of informality, as anywhere else. He never acts as if he owns the place. When he sits himself down in an armchair he has probably sat in a hundred times before, it's as if he was sitting in any old armchair in some godforsaken hotel at the end of the world. Whether he pours himself a drink, prepares a dish or crosses a room, it's as if he was in a house he had rented for the duration of the holidays and will never see again. This distance from things and from memories of the past pleases Anna greatly. She herself has always loathed revisiting the past. Whenever she finds herself surrounded by the furnishings and fabrics of her childhood, she tries desperately to keep them at bay, to depersonalize them and see them as wholly alien to herself. Nothing could be more abhorrent in her eyes than objects having a sentimental value. Not that Thomas Lenz is an abstraction; no, he really does have this bladelike body that opens up the town like a piece of fruit. But like Anna—and it's not the first thing they have in common—there can be no question of his allying himself to the past.

Yes, they share the same masked horror of the past. They both keep up appearances, for to have the upper hand you must deceive the enemy continually, it's the only way; to meet him face to face is quite impossible, you would lose. They both pretend, therefore, to retain a tenderhearted interest in the past, there are even times when they themselves are taken in, they know exactly—how skilled they have become from all those years of caution!—how to defuse the past by having it self-destruct in their mind. And so they can allude to their childhood as if it had been a natural one. It's a wise move, moreover, as we all have need of an imagined childhood. She also likes his way of not touching things; and when he does touch them, of acting as if they had no soul. It's from resemblances such as these that unbridled love is sometimes forged. The bedsheets don't really interest him, neither do the blankets, he no longer knows where they're kept in fact, the beds are unfamiliar and the rooms unvisited, he's quite happy just showing Anna the house he used to live in, and she is, too, moving about in his dream as if it were her own.

Thanks to that visit, the bond between them has been reinforced. They can find no words for this, and as a matter of fact there *are* no words for it. It's not that the thing from the past is so horrific that it leaves you speechless. No, it's more subtle than that: the thing from the past is indistinct, vague, bodiless. To tell the truth, the thing from the past is unformed. But what had always been complicated for both of them was that it had no name. It wasn't a violence done to their bodies; it was more like a violence done to their consciousness. Something had scarred their consciousness. That's why Anna Lore, when she saw Thomas Lenz coming toward her in the street in Sorge in August 2002, immediately fell in love with him; and why Thomas Lenz found her so arresting all of a sudden. The mystery, the only mystery, is that you can recognize that scar in someone who has yet to open their mouth. It must reside in the body, therefore. It must also be manifest in their very presence. Is it because someone looks peculiarly insulated even when chatting with other people? Perhaps. Thomas maintained that before, when he would see Anna walking by in Sorge (for he had already noticed her), he had been struck by how cold and distant she was. "Not at all," protests Anna, "how could you possibly find me cold and distant? I love running into old acquaintances in Sorge, I always go over and engage them in lively, cheerful conversation." "I don't know," he says, "I found you icy."

And what about him? No, he definitely hadn't been

icy; he'd been courteous and friendly, as she herself could be when she didn't feel anything—especially when she didn't feel anything. When she didn't feel anything, as was often the case, she was the most delightful woman in the world: attentive, affectionate, high-spirited. But if she felt something, she could be twice as attentive, affectionate and high-spirited—precisely in order to stop feeling, to cover it over and hush it up. "Which is why I'm usually so exquisite," she says to Thomas with a laugh. He laughs, too. He sees exactly what she means. They study each other like two animals of the same species, each fully aware of the other's resources, of their strange and, as it were, counterfeit vulnerability and their capacity to turn tail all of a sudden. Guillaume as a child of the sun was extremely impressive, but Thomas is even more so, for he's not afraid to lose. Their bodies don't touch as they walk untiringly through the streets of Bordeaux, but every now and then—at a concert, for example—their hands are so tightly clasped, their wrists and forearms so hopelessly entwined, that you would think they were clinging to each other, as if at the prospect or in recollection of a disaster. Everyone must think them charming, these lovers who are so deeply in love. And to tell the truth, they are.

She longs to be with him the way you might lie in a river and let the waters wash over you and play between your limbs, and slide across your belly and neck, while slender fish ply between your legs and dart across your thighs, soft weeds caress you, your hair is adrift, overhead are marvelous branches with bright green leaves, and even higher up a hard but bright blue sky, and the stones beneath the water might almost be made of flesh. They would follow the river upstream like two skiffs, two bodies famed in the annals of love; she thinks of the Risée, the big river near Sorge whose harsh banks are formed of great, brutal black boulders, but whose waters are so clear and low that you can wade across them at times almost without getting your knees wet. But why dream of drowning and drifting away like this? No, no, Anna tells herself, as she gazes out of the window at the garden, it has nothing to do with drowning. On the contrary, it's about surrendering to the flow of things at last, with this man who is not Jude the Obscure but Thomas Lenz, who has a real body of very handsome flesh, whose eyes laugh now and then, and more and more often, in fact, and whose left hand doesn't have a wedding ring.

She would like to buy him a bracelet. A tiny, barely visible bond enclosing the slim brown wrist which had made such a powerful impression on her the first time she saw him. He probably wouldn't like that, for he's the man in the world the most averse to signs. She would like to offer him gifts—she, who has never known what to offer a man. But she still thinks of Guillaume from time to time, in his pride, with his eagle's head in the snow and the considerable warmth of his body, which he had placed at her disposal for all those days and nights all those years. She's appalled that he should be receding into the past, this man she had loved so much, and would love like that, she had thought, until the end of their days. Is he, too, starting to forget her to quite this degree? "I will always love you," she had told him when they had parted. "Of course you won't," he had replied, "everything is forgotten, it happens very fast in fact." So she still thinks of him from time to time, but deliberately now, as if in shame for a task she has neglected, out of loyalty and devotion to his memory. She sees him on a flight of steps outside an oratory in Naples, where they had wandered without realizing it into a rather dangerous neighborhood; in the heat of Pompeii, which was almost deserted that day; among the ruins of Selinunte in Sicily; and it hurts her to think of him as if all that was truly ended, truly behind them. But his voice on the phone has changed. It's no longer the same man, it's no longer the Guillaume who loved her; a chill has crept into his voice that wasn't there before, and when he says to her: "Do you recognize my voice?," "Of course I do, I haven't become an amnesiac, you know," she replies fondly, with a laugh. And yet, for a split second, it's true, she hadn't recognized this voice which had left her only a few months ago, this voice which had spoken to her, dandled her, sustained her, played with her and danced with her every hour of every day for twenty years.

Are we so familiar with grief and death, then, that we can draw a line that swiftly through all we have experienced? Or is it just Anna Lore, with her aversion to remembering, who, having twice lost someone she loved, has learned not to wait around or look back? In the cemetery where the two women lie, she places poppies, gentians, and sometimes buttercups on their grave. On the headstone now and then she runs her finger over the letters of their names and the dates of their births and deaths, sealed boxes of forty-three years containing their lives, their thoughts, everything they experienced and felt and touched. She doesn't feel much in the presence of the gleaming low vault, other than a sense of having lost her way somewhat in this garden. Sometimes she runs into her sister Laure there, likewise come to pay her respects; they wave to each other from opposite ends of the cemetery. It's the only real relationship they have, in fact: waving to each other across the graves. They walk quietly toward each other along the grassy pathways, Laure picks a mallow, Anna rights a vase, "The wind's getting up," says Laure, "Yes, aren't those red flowers pretty," asks Anna, and running their hands over the warm gravestones, together they leave the garden of the dead through a gate that has been creaking in exactly the same manner ever since their childhood.

Guillaume, she thinks to herself, Guillaume, where have you gone? How could you abandon me? But it's done now. He had said to her: when you told me you loved someone else, something in me shattered. At the time, she had thought it was bad literature, one of those stock responses you come out with when you don't really know what's happening to you. But it's probably true. It's possible, in fact, that even before she had made her confession, in the black and white woods where he had suddenly had the head of an eagle, it was all over. Yes, it was the eagle head that had marked the end, like the full stop after the final word in a book. After that come the needless repetitions, the attempts at carrying on, the desire to go further, to keep trying, for no one likes to abandon a book they're writing, you want to abide there, to be in that river forever. It was so beautiful to have found it, so unhoped-for, so grandiose. It's not every day you find a book to write, a love affair to experience. In general, they're things that elude you, you spend your time chasing after them, saddened to be exiled. Guillaume's book had begun when he had turned up twenty years ago in Anna's dining room, in a navy-blue suit he had never owned, and ended in the snow the day they didn't know how to speak to each other any more. A book vast and deep like a bed filled with odors—a book of prayer, a sort of Bible or Old Testament—while the book of Thomas was the New.

AND SO THEY ADVANCE toward each other, Anna Lore and Thomas Lenz. No longer does he simply appear out of nowhere. In a sort of boundless landscape they have made their own, they arrive at last, reaching out to one another across the divide. Around them are drums and music. How could she ever have mistaken him for Jude the Obscure! He doesn't look a bit like Jude the Obscure, for heaven's sake! For one thing, he's made of human flesh and has a heart, he has given her ample proof of this over the last ten months, he laughs and says the most amusing things, with a laughter that comes from afar and had struck Anna when she heard it for the very first time in bed. To keep out the cold, he wraps a long scarf she has given him around his neck, he's a little less reserved than in the past, and his trousers are not so extraordinary after all, though what is concealed beneath them is. He has a sex that bleeds. Whenever he's unhappy, his sex bleeds. Like the wound of the Fisher King. And his sex bleeds sometimes (only sometimes) since meeting Anna. Before, it never bled. He sees doctors, takes tests, everything is fine: no lesions, no infection, no organic disorder. No one understands a thing. Moreover, when he's happy with Anna and Anna loves him, he doesn't bleed. It's when she leaves him, when she wants to break off, that something happens to his body in his sleep, and he wakes up bleeding.

Is this what she had sensed when she had thought their two wounds a perfect match? She had never imagined, of course, that the match would prove quite so eloquent. And yet from the very outset, ever since their second coffee in Sorge in August 2002, she had been intrigued by that sex—not as an instrument of pleasure but as if it concealed Thomas's secret, as if Thomas's secret was located there. Taken aback and not a little alarmed by these outbreaks, Thomas still keeps a cool head. He doesn't panic. He observes. It's Anna who is alarmed, Anna who wants him to see a specialist—but a specialist of what? Of wounds? Thomas isn't cut out for therapy. No, she thinks to herself, apart from my caresses and kisses, apart from contact with my body, only literature can treat this disease. So she gives him books to read, and the effusion stops. Not any old books, of course, but books written in a state of mind such that they cauterize. Thomas, however, requires more and more books, more and more often. Week after week, favorite books are dispatched from her bookshelves in Sorge, where she continues to live, to Bordeaux. The moment his work is done and he has left the center where he has spent the day investigating crimes, Thomas goes home to read, astonished to discover the good it does him. Piotr Sengel and Alexandre Ider do him a world of good. Tommaso Ordoli falls wide of the mark. (It's strange, she would have thought Ordoli perfect for the job. Apparently not.) With Effie Karane or Marie des Fossés, the bleeding stops at the very first sentence. Of the thousand books on her shelves, Anna realizes, perhaps only fifty can put a stop to a hemorrhage that has no discernible scientific cause.

Will she be dealing with a man who is sickly, then? No more so than she is, though she'll need to care for him, no doubt, just as Guillaume had cared for her with his tenderness and love. Anna had never been much of a nurse, but perhaps that silly old saying according to which you must one day give back what you have received was not so silly after all. She remains on her guard, however: she wouldn't want

Thomas to have somehow sensed this taste she has for healing and, playing on it, to have unwittingly shed that blood merely in order to bind her to him. Vulnerability is often the worst kind of blackmail. Flee the depressed; they tap into your energy only to relieve you of it. They couldn't care less about your strength; they envy you for it and hate you for being happy. But Thomas isn't like that. She sees him crossing the desert to reach her, his blue scarf knotted around his neck, his dusky features parched by the wind and sand and sun. He could easily have died all alone there, he wouldn't have broadcast the fact. He's so accustomed to solitude and stone, with just the occasional oasis now and then, that he might almost have been happier in the desert than in the arms of love. Fevers frequently rise and fall in him at the speed of a rifle shot, like that outrageous fairground attraction in Bordeaux; fevers that, if not quite purposeless, themselves have no discernible cause. There are times when he's sleeping when he almost looks like he's dead.

But isn't their love itself like that rifle shot in Bordeaux? They have only to hear their voices on the phone for fevers to rise and fall in them with a savagery and speed that astounds them. The moment they make contact—at the mere sounds of their voices but also because she's talking to Jude the Obscure, and he to God-knows-whom; to an image, too, no doubt—they feel a burning desire, not so much to sleep together as to touch each other, even when they are dressed. "What I would really love," says Anna, "is for you to arrive, and then, while you still have your jacket on, for me to slip my hand inside and touch your waist and hip through your shirt. It's all I want at this point. It might even be all I want *period*. The rest, you see, is almost incidental. Forgive me, but touching your body, touching you there—and I don't know why there in particular—is basically all I want, all I could possibly wish for; it's as if touching you had been so impossible, as it were, that gaining access to that spot is quite incredible in itself." "For my part," he says, "I want first of all to see you, that's the most important thing; and then next, to hear you, and then to feel you. The rest will also come later, but it's less important, as it were, forgive me. Seeing you is already an event in itself. Perhaps at that point the fever will pass," he says. "It'll be a relief because it's tiresome feeling feverish like this all the time, but if it passes because I touch you I'll be furious with myself. In that case, I really have no control over anything."

She laughs. She's waiting for him. He'll turn up in his tweed jacket or another one, he'll look remarkably self-possessed, he won't jump on her, on the contrary—O wonder of wonders!—he won't move. Instead, she'll be the one pressing up against him, as if he had no hands or arms. Guillaume, for heaven's sake, was like Shiva, with his thousand arms and thousand phalluses! She'll touch Thomas's side at the exact spot where Christ was pierced, for if Guillaume was God the Father, Thomas is quite obviously the Son, and at the moment of contact he'll throw his head back and cry out. Is that love or is it a form of madness? He'll fold her in his voice, they'll sleep together, but it'll be nothing like sleeping with Guillaume, with the marvelous pleasures it held in store. Sleeping with Thomas is something else entirely, as she had explained to Guillaume, who hadn't understood. There are times when it feels as if they were reverting to the hardships of childhood, but what happens there is so grave, they are amazed and at the same time so grief-stricken, so sad and yet so happy to have found each other, that it's like a secret ceremony where you do things in a dream. Already their first time together she had felt he had this Christlike body, but had dismissed the notion as too simple, too facile, and no doubt masking some other, more interesting image. She had mentioned it to him, however, and he had gone through the roof—indignant, outraged by this dubious, sacrilegious comparison.

He has in him a groundswell of irritation never openly acknowledged as such but always there, rumbling in the background, like the rumor of the city in an apartment, or the sound of the blood in your veins during a Doppler exam. She had heard it during their first coffees together in Sorge in that second summer, in August 2003, and it was this she had been listening to while they were chatting about the people of Sorge or their own occupations and the books they were reading. Was it rage? Anna wondered. A perfectly contained violence that might one day erupt? She saw him as a volcano, with an active, simmering interior. No, he said, I promise you, there's no rage in me. But she didn't believe him, she thought he probably didn't know exactly what he had inside him. No one has a body as compact, lean and taut as that, like box or olive wood, unless they are holding something firmly in place. "That's just literature," he had said, to needle her. But Anna was old enough to know that when people said "literature" it was because something was true and had wounded them slightly. While they were both smoking their fifth cigarette side by side at the Café des Alizés, gazing out over a square where lanterns were being hung for a ball, she visited this body seated next to hers, this body that was such a novelty in her life. She compared it to others. Philippe, the cobbler whom she would sometimes chat with, likewise had a slim, taut body, but, unlike Thomas's, it didn't have that rumor in it, that hue and cry. As for Guillaume's body, it was a deep, still forest, vast in extent and very tall, in which you would suddenly hear the clacking of a bird's wings as it flew up or changed branches.

While Thomas is making his way toward her, Anna Lore dreams over and over again, for in a few pages it will be time to step down from her reverie, and what a pity that will be. The nearer he draws to her, the closer they come to the end of this tale of a woman torn in two, and the more she talks about it to others—at all hours of the day, with everyone. Never has she been quite so eager for her story to be set down in the trees, the stones, the grass, in the minds and bodies of those around her. Yesterday she dined with Pierre at a friend's house. It was warm out, they had sat for a long time in the garden, the sky overhead was orange, a tortoise was making its way slowly across the lawn, creamy, pale-yellow roses were climbing up the walls and she was thinking about Guillaume because on their way to the house they had stopped at a service station where she had bought some candy as she had done a hundred times with Guillaume when they were driving around together. Her heart grew heavy, then all at once flooded with sorrow, washing back and forth, ebbing away, then returning again. Even the gate to the house was painful to her because they had passed in front of a similar gate one day when Guillaume was standing in the road telephoning someone while she strolled around, waiting for him. The garden, which was beautifully laid out and opened onto a cornfield with a steeple in the distance, introduced a further note of sadness. She had been so radiant for twenty years: there had been nothing in her past to regret, not a single image to mar her joy. Had she gone mad, turning her back on joy in exchange for a wound? How can you turn your back on joy? Isn't it diabolical, perverse, a violation of the natural order, to turn your back on joy in exchange for a wound? Isn't the usual movement of a life in the opposite direction? Walking with the mistress of the house and her friends in the garden set with stone benches in a semicircle and trembling tall cherry trees, she shuddered for a second at the thought of the horror she had accomplished. Will she henceforth look on everything beautiful, harmonious, and peaceful as though in mourning for the paradise she has lost? Is she doomed never to be happy in that way again? Is it not the height of folly to deliberately turn your back on happiness?

She's also a bit scared of Guillaume. Revealing his underside in the pain that had taken hold of him, he had made a strange remark, which was moving around inside her like a little snake. He had told her—it was scarcely credible, it was appalling that Guillaume could say or think such a thing—that he wished her ill. And yet so close was the bond between them that, regardless of circumstances and events, regardless of the tall trees in her friends' garden and the roofs of Bordeaux and Paris and Sorge, and the thousand streets and all those roads and woods and fields, anything Guillaume felt Anna felt, too, and anything Anna felt would affect him, too. Were Guillaume to wish Anna ill, therefore—should he wish her to feel pain, wish her life to grow dark, without hope or joy or gaiety—that wish would circulate throughout Anna's body. But surely he can't have suffered so much as to feel a lasting hatred for her, can he? She thinks of him in Rousseau's garden at Les Charmettes, near Chambéry, he wouldn't stop photographing her, which had annoyed her and made her laugh; later, near Annecy, the car engine had caught fire, and they had lunched by the lake and then gone in search of a garage; the world was his oyster, wherever he happened to be he would land on his feet, set to work, cook up a surprise, invent something, change roads. No, a heart like that can't possibly... Still, she fears him because he's powerful. Evil, certainly not. But like anyone under the circumstances, were the pain to persist he might put off his kingly attire.

You can combat pretty much anything in life, but there's one thing you cannot take arms against, and that is the evil eye. If the evil eye is on you, you have no chance of escape. A good many lives that seem inexplicably bleak and subterranean, unspeakably tormented, owe their undoing perhaps to this eye observing them and wishing them ill. The evil eye of someone who has loved you deeply and has been deeply wounded can cast a pall over your existence, or something more terrible still. Guillaume needed to remember, however, that Anna was not as young as she was, was no longer the capering flame she had been at the beginning, was not even all that desirable perhaps, and that her stomach pains and her constant need of stimulation and entertainment could be a bit burdensome at times. Was Anna really deserving of all this lamentation? Wasn't it just her type of personality that was so captivating? Released from her spell, didn't one have a truer sense of existence, as it were? She set your mind wandering, because her own mind wandered so much; but in the midst of all that celebrating, didn't one long sometimes for a more authentic relationship? One less archaic and whimsical and more attuned to the realities of life? True, they would go and sit at the top of the Rocher Saint-Anne, and there she would graze on the grass—like a cow, she said, "I want to know what it feels like to be a cow." A woman like that is fun to be with, she connects you to the earth and sky, and when she's gone everything seems clear-cut and cold once more. But after a while, doesn't one feel something truer to life and more authentic establishing itself in your existence? Can a life without sorrow really be called a life?

Tomorrow, Thomas will be here in the house in Sorge that Guillaume has abandoned. He has been so feverish this last month, day after day, without break—and yet "I promise you," he says, "I don't feel pain anywhere, I even have a healthy appetite, my head just feels a bit heavy, especially at night"; "Do you shiver at all?" she asks; "No," he says, "there's no shivering"—that she wonders what this body at her door will feel like. Burning? With the desire to see her, yes, certainly, as she is to see him. It's not every day, after all, that, stepping out of a book—and a very beautiful book, too—Jude the Obscure comes knocking at your door; and that, on touching him, you touch a dream. She'll fold him in her arms like a child. He'd been so mistreated all those years ago, Jude the Obscure: she'll look after him. In bed at night he'll have his boyish eyes and his fits of laughter, a little disconcerting at first for a woman who had thought she was dealing with a mysterious vigilante from the Wild West, a watchmaker who sold hourglasses and water clocks, a murdered Russian poet. But she's got the picture now. Lying in her bed is a boy of twelve, joyous and a little scared, who doesn't have a clue what's going on but who once dreamed with his crazy best friend who would later kill himself of some day meeting a woman who would say, yes, yes, yes, and embrace him. It's incredible, he says. She laughs.